ENTANGLED

Center Point
Large Print

Also by J. S. Scott and available from
Center Point Large Print:

Ensnared

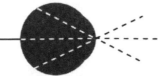

**This Large Print Book carries the
Seal of Approval of N.A.V.H.**

ENTANGLED

**THE
ACCIDENTAL
BILLIONAIRES**

BOOK TWO

J. S. SCOTT

CENTER POINT LARGE PRINT
THORNDIKE, MAINE

This book is dedicated to my husband, Sri, who does so much for me every single day. He works behind the scenes. He does most of the cooking and a great deal of the technical stuff for my books. He leads the team and makes sure that a lot of the nonwriting stuff gets done when I'm on a deadline. There aren't many men who would just pick up and work with their wives to help their careers. He's an unsung hero to me, and critical to the success of my books. Thanks for all that you do, Sri. What would I do without you?

All my love,
Jan

ENTANGLED

PROLOGUE
Skye

Nine years ago . . .

"I love you," I murmured to Aiden Sinclair as he held me tightly against his body in another good-bye hug that was breaking my heart.

The fact that I'd just said *those words* probably surprised me more than it did Aiden.

After all, I'd given him my virginity over the summer we'd spent together, so he had to know that he made me feel things I'd never experienced before.

He was a piece of myself that had always been missing. I just hadn't known it until he'd started to look at me like I was *his,* like we belonged *together*.

I'm not a romantic. Far from it. Maybe I *was* only eighteen years old, but I'd had to grow up early, and my life was far from a fairy tale. The only exception had been the time I'd spent with Aiden over this magical summer that was now coming to an end.

Reluctantly, I let go of the tight grip I had around his neck as he pulled back. But I was rewarded by seeing the face of the man I loved more than I'd ever loved anyone.

His beautiful blue eyes studied me as he said huskily, "I'll miss you, sweetheart. But I'll be back in a little over eight weeks. Are you going to be okay?"

For a moment, I was disappointed that he hadn't told me that he loved me, too. But maybe it was just too soon for him.

Not that I didn't want to hear those words *right now,* but we had only been dating for a couple of months.

I shot him a small smile. "Of course. Are you afraid I'm not going to wait for you? If you are, I have to tell you that you've kind of ruined me for any other guy."

Aiden and I joked like that. We'd started off the summer as friends. His sister Jade, my best friend, had left for the university early, right after our high-school graduation. And yeah, I'd seen Aiden around, but I was pretty sure he'd taken pity on me once his sister had left, and hung out with me because I'd missed Jade so much. Not that the insane attraction between us hadn't been there at the beginning of the summer, but he hadn't acted on it until recently.

"Stay safe," he demanded.

I nodded. Aiden knew my background. And it was no secret in Citrus Beach that my mother was eccentric, which was a nice way of saying she was actually certifiable at times.

"I'll be fine," I reassured him. Aiden was overly

protective, but it was kind of nice because I'd actually never had anybody who worried about me or my safety. It was . . . comforting. He made me feel safe. "I'm starting classes in a couple of days."

Unlike Aiden's little sister, I *hadn't* gotten an amazing scholarship at a prestigious college, so I'd settled for taking classes at our local junior college. But I was okay with that. I wasn't gifted like Jade was, and I didn't aspire to huge heights for my future. I just wanted a job I liked so I could get the hell away from my lunatic mother. And I knew I needed an education or trade to truly break away from her and the insanity in our house. Southern California wasn't a cheap place to live, so getting a decent job that actually paid well was a must.

"I wish your mother would pay you for working your ass off at her restaurant," Aiden grumbled.

I shifted and leaned back against his hard body. We were saying good-bye at the local park, taking a whole bench to ourselves. Since it was very early in the morning, there weren't many people in the public place. There was nobody else in sight.

His arms wrapped around me from behind, and I let out a sigh of contentment as I rested my head against his chest, wishing he *wasn't* due to leave for an eight-week commercial fishing job within the next fifteen minutes. But I knew he was doing it for his family. He still had a younger brother and sisters to support.

I'd never met a man who worked as hard as Aiden did for his family. Maybe that was partially the reason I'd fallen for him so hard.

Finally, I answered him. "In my mother's mind, she *does* pay me. She feeds me, and she lets me live in her house."

"That's bullshit," he rumbled. "You're her goddamn daughter, not her slave."

"I just have to deal with it for a couple of years," I explained to him patiently. "Once I finish the nursing program, I'll be able to get out on my own. It's not a problem, Aiden. Really, it's not."

I'd dealt with my mother my entire life. I could handle a couple more years. I'd just have to keep thinking about the future instead of dwelling on how much I needed to get out of crazy town. I didn't have a whole lot of choice.

Yes, I'd worked in my mother's run-down café for years, but since I wasn't an employee, I technically had no work experience. What I needed was an *education*. Even if I *could* land a waitressing job that paid, I couldn't support myself on that income, or go to school to get a job that would get me out of my mother's home for good.

As long as I was living with my mother, I'd be forced to continue being her free labor.

But it was a means to a much happier end if I could finally be free.

"Baby, if I wasn't so goddamn poor—"

"Stop," I interrupted him. "I'm *not* your responsibility, Aiden."

God knew he had *way too many* of those as it was. He and his two older brothers, Noah and Seth, had held their family together and raised their three younger siblings. To me, he was a hero who'd put his own needs aside for his family for years. I didn't want him putting himself down. *Ever.* Being poor wasn't something he should be ashamed of. Keeping the Sinclair family together, in spite of the fact that they didn't have much money, should make him proud.

Aiden and I had both grown up poor. Maybe that was why we understood each other so well.

"I *want* you to be my responsibility, sweetheart. I want you to be mine," he said in a low, dangerous tone that always made me melt. "I know you're probably too damn young for me, but I've given up fighting that."

There was a six-year age gap between us, but it wasn't something we'd ever really noticed. I was pretty sure we were both old souls and had acted like adults for as long as we could remember.

"I am yours," I told him. "But that doesn't mean you have to *support me*. My *heart* is yours."

I turned and put my palm against the scruff

13

on his jaw, trying to make him understand that I didn't want to ever be a burden to him. He'd sacrificed so much. I just wanted to be *with him*.

Seeing the conflict in his gorgeous eyes made my heart ache.

"Your heart better be mine, because I'm not letting you go," he finally grumbled as his head swooped down to capture my mouth.

The feel of his gorgeous, hot, silken lips on mine set my body on fire. As usual, it started with an electric spark between my thighs that turned into roaring flames within seconds.

I wanted to claim this man as mine right now.

I wanted to know he'd always be with me.

I wanted so much more than just an intense summer romance.

I knew I'd have to wait. Aiden's family would come first until they were all raised and educated. I loved him for his family loyalty and drive to see all of his siblings independent. So I was more than willing to tamp down my instincts until he was free of those obligations. Aiden was worth it.

I wasn't going anywhere.

And I still wanted so many things for my own future, too.

My hands fisted in his gloriously coarse, thick dark hair as he nibbled at my lips and then claimed my mouth all over again.

My heart was racing as he finally pulled back and grinned at me.

"Eight weeks seems like a long time right now, baby."

God, I loved that naughty, mischievous expression on his face.

I nodded. "I'm going to miss you so much," I said honestly.

He rested his forehead against mine. "I'll miss you, too, sweetheart. Take care of yourself."

He rose and pulled me to my feet. "I have to go. Think about me while I'm gone. Fuck knows I'll be thinking about you. I want to give you something before I go."

I looked at him with curiosity. "What? I thought you already gave me *that* last night," I teased.

He shot me a warning look as he dug into the pocket of his jeans. "Don't remind me, or you're going to get *that* again, too."

Like I'd mind if he dragged me somewhere private and we said good-bye with our bodies one more time? I honestly craved it. But I knew he had to be in San Diego on time.

"I want you to have this," he said as he slipped something over my head. "My mother didn't have a lot of jewelry, but we all got something when she died. It's just a red tiger's-eye stone. But I want you to keep it."

Our eyes met, and my heart skittered as I realized he was giving me something that had belonged to his mother, who had died years ago.

Something precious to him.

I rarely cried, but tears sprang to my eyes, and a droplet escaped to roll down my cheek. I clutched the small stone that was hanging around my neck by a delicate chain. "I've never had a piece of jewelry," I said, my heart in my throat.

"It looks good on you," he said with a wink.

I threw myself into his arms and plastered my body against his. Every tumultuous emotion I was experiencing was very close to the surface.

I didn't want him to go.

I wanted to keep our bodies close, and keep exploring the intense emotions that Aiden always brought out in me.

And I wanted to keep feeling as cherished and as safe as I had for most of the summer.

But I finally let go because I knew I had to. "Go," I insisted, even as my heart screamed for him to stay. "Thank you for the gift. I'll keep it safe."

He kissed me one more time, and then pressed a kiss to my forehead. "See ya soon, sweetheart."

"Be careful," I called as he turned and started to make his way to his truck.

"Always," he bellowed back. "I have a lot to come home to."

I swiped the tears that started to fall harder as I watched his retreating figure disappear.

Home. He'll be back home soon. Eight weeks isn't all that long, right?

I collapsed on the bench, my legs shaky, and I

realized that I had a death grip on the stone Aiden had given me.

He'd left something important to him behind with me. It was enough to keep me believing he'd come back.

I tucked the small red tiger's-eye inside my T-shirt and then stood back up. I needed to get home, or I'd catch hell from my mother.

I'd never told her about my relationship with Aiden, because I knew she wouldn't approve. She'd never liked any of the Sinclair family, even though Jade had been my best friend for years.

Funny how my mother's opinion didn't matter all that much to me anymore.

I knew Aiden.

Our souls were connected. I could feel it.

I loved him.

And *that* was all that mattered.

I started jogging toward my house, wearing a silly grin on my face because I could feel the stone he'd given me against my skin as I made my way back home.

CHAPTER 1
Skye

The present . . .

My heart sank as I realized there was only one seat available at the dinner table.

That's what I get for running late. Shit! Shit! Shit!

Every chair was taken except the one next to *him*.

Aiden Sinclair.

The man I'd been trying to avoid ever since I'd come back to Citrus Beach, California, permanently with my daughter, Maya.

He was the thorn in my side.

He was the only part of moving home, after almost a decade away, that I hated.

He was dangerous.

And I never let myself forget that for even a moment.

I sighed in resignation as I looked around the enormous table—like I was suddenly going to see another vacant place.

Not going to happen. My timing and my luck had never been all that good, so why should that change now?

"Come sit next to Aiden, Skye," my best friend, Jade Sinclair, requested from her spot next to her billionaire fiancé, Eli Stone.

Jade and Eli were the reason I was here. The *only* reason. We were two weeks away from their wedding ceremony, and this was an impromptu get-together for everyone involved in planning the festivities or included in the wedding party. Eli's home in Citrus Beach had been the logical place to meet up, since his house was bigger than Jade's.

Honestly, almost everyone here had the last name of Sinclair except for Jade's fiancé; Eli's mother; Jade's twin sister, Brooke, since she was wedded to Liam Sullivan now; and . . . me.

I was *still* Skye Weston, even though I'd been married and divorced. I'd changed my name back to my maiden name soon after my ex-husband had been put in prison for life.

I looked around the table again, amazed that one family could take up so much space. I was the only child of a mother who had been a single parent; the Sinclair family was so different from my own.

I'd been an only child, a lonely kid.

Even now, my daughter was really all I had.

How could a family *this size* not take up a lot of room? Jade had four brothers and a twin sister. Her half-siblings, cousins, and a bunch of other family hadn't even shown up yet from the East Coast, and the large dining room was full.

I started making my way slowly down the table reluctantly after I shot a fake smile at Jade. I didn't want her to know that sitting next to Aiden would be torture for me.

"Sorry I'm late," I said in a voice loud enough to carry to my best friend. "I got hung up at the restaurant."

When *wasn't* I delayed by work at the Weston Café? I'd put every available moment and penny into getting the little diner I'd inherited from my deceased mother to turn a profit.

The only thing *more important* than work was my daughter, Maya.

I finally sat my ass down and smiled at Seth, another one of Jade's older brothers, who was sitting on my left.

I completely avoided looking to my right, since I was determined to ignore Aiden.

"How are you doing, Skye?" Seth queried politely.

"I'm good," I lied.

I'd be doing a lot better if I wasn't forced into sitting next to Aiden.

I hated myself for the fact that I could *feel* Aiden's presence, and that just a whiff of his masculine scent made my body suddenly come alive after a very long absence of experiencing any kind of desire.

I can't show any reaction. I can't.

I momentarily contemplated asking Seth if he

21

wanted to change seats, but I knew it would look childish. The last thing I wanted was for Aiden to know that he bothered me *at all*.

It was exactly two weeks until Jade and Eli's wedding, and it wouldn't be the only time Aiden and I would have to be in close proximity to each other. But it was only fourteen days. For the most part, I'd managed to stay out of his company since I'd returned to Citrus Beach almost a year ago . . . *until today*.

"You look exhausted," Aiden commented gruffly. "But you smell like fresh lemon. How does that happen?"

I chastised myself silently for the shiver that slithered down my spine from hearing the sound of Aiden's sexy baritone. Grudgingly, I turned my head toward him. "Lemon supreme pie was the special today," I snapped.

It was embarrassing that I hadn't had time to go home and wash the smell of citrus fruit from my skin, and change out of the jeans and T-shirt I'd worked in all day. But I'd already been late getting here.

"It wasn't a criticism," he answered huskily. "You smell good. Lemon pie is my favorite."

"I know," I said automatically, and then wanted to kick myself for remembering.

My brief relationship with Aiden had ended almost a decade ago. Shouldn't I have forgotten all that minor stuff?

"Someday, you're going to have to explain why you hate me so much," Aiden said in a low voice as he leaned in close to my ear.

I looked around the table. There were so many conversations happening, and being at a table composed mostly of Sinclairs was deafening. Nobody was paying the least bit of attention to us.

Honestly, I had plenty of reasons to hate Aiden. "You know exactly why," I said sharply back at him. "Let's not go there right now, okay?"

I had to get a grip. I needed to retain control. I *could not* let Aiden Sinclair shake the facade of coolness that I'd worked so hard to acquire.

"I *need* to go there," he argued in an infuriatingly calm tone. "It's been over nine years, Skye. We had a great summer fling. Yeah, it didn't end well. But it's been over for a long time."

Dishes filled with food were being passed around the table, but I handed most of them on without taking much on my plate. I was nauseated just because I was in such close proximity to Aiden. He made me nervous. But I was actually *forced* to talk to him to avoid being noticeably rude.

I refuse to disappoint Jade. I can't.

We were getting close to the day of my best friend's wedding. Jade was so happy. I could suffer through whatever I had to endure to not make a scene.

I'd been back in Citrus Beach for almost a year. Fortunately, I'd avoided getting anywhere near Aiden—for the most part, anyway. Yeah, we'd had a few encounters, but I'd always been able to walk away.

Right now, I was a captive. It was either make myself speak to him, or screw up the dinner.

Not a difficult choice since Jade's happiness was important to me.

"It *has* been a long time," I agreed in a voice that sounded bitchy to my own ears. "Let's just drop it. We can be cordial."

Liar. I'm such a liar.

Cordial wasn't a demeanor that worked very well with Aiden, even now.

He wasn't the type of guy to make polite conversation.

I hadn't had a real conversation with Aiden since he'd left at the end of the summer, over nine years ago, for an eight-week commercial-fishing gig. Maybe my anger should have been gone, but it wasn't. And it was pretty damn hard to pretend that what had happened didn't matter anymore.

He probably shouldn't have been able to rattle me, but there were plenty of reasons that he did.

"You need to eat something." Aiden added a large pile of mashed potatoes to my plate without asking, and then smothered it with gravy.

I glared at him. "I didn't want that much."

He shrugged. "It's your favorite. And you have next to nothing on your plate."

I opened my mouth to say something else, but I promptly closed it again.

How in the hell had he remembered that I could make a meal out of mashed potatoes?

"I'm not that hungry," I answered.

Really, my stomach was rolling.

I started to eat, hoping it might calm my upset stomach, but I couldn't help but watch Aiden out of the corner of my eye as he devoured the massive pile of food he'd amassed on his own plate.

Aiden Sinclair hadn't *always* been a billionaire like he was now. In fact, the Sinclair family in California had always been incredibly poor— just like my mother and I had been when I was younger.

Aiden and I had shared a common bond because neither one of us had ever had any money.

But God, had Aiden's fortunes changed since we'd last talked to each other nine years ago.

He'd inherited massive wealth. He and all of his siblings had, including my best friend, Jade.

I, on the other hand, had . . . not.

For most of his adult life, Aiden had been a commercial fisherman. He'd spent long periods of time out at sea, burning so many calories that he could barely manage to keep enough in to maintain his incredibly muscular build.

Apparently, he was *still* making up for all those lost calories.

He nodded at my plate. "Eat," he said, making it sound like an order instead of a request.

I ignored him and reached for one of the many bottles of wine sitting on the table instead, filling my glass nearly to the brim before I slugged half of it down.

I can do this. It's just dinner. I can ignore Aiden. I don't have to react.

I dug into the mountain of mashed potatoes, knowing the sooner I finished, the quicker I could excuse myself.

Unfortunately, Seth was involved in another conversation, so I couldn't talk to him. So I chose to occupy myself with getting some food down.

Aiden was silent until he'd cleaned his plate.

"The café is looking better," he said in a casual tone once he'd placed his fork on his empty plate.

I pushed my half-eaten food forward. I was done. "Thank you," I answered stiffly. "It needed some improvements."

I'd done a ton of cosmetic work on the building. It had been pretty outdated, so I'd been doing some painting and décor work on my own. My mother had let everything go for years before her sudden death from a heart attack. I hadn't known how bad things really were until I'd moved from San Diego to Citrus Beach to take over the café after she'd passed away.

"Did you have to do it all yourself? You really do look tired." Aiden's attention was suddenly focused entirely on me.

I took a deep breath. "There was no money in my mother's estate to do it. So yes, I had to save as much as possible on repairs and improvements."

I wasn't about to tell Aiden that I'd barely scratched the surface. The building where the restaurant was housed was old and needed a hell of a lot more than paint.

"Weren't you married to a rich guy?"

My ex-husband, Marco, *had been* a wealthy man . . . until he and his entire Mafia family had ended up in prison for life. "We're divorced," I said sharply. "And criminals don't usually get to keep the money they stole from other people."

"Then maybe you shouldn't have run off with him in the first place. You were too damn young to be married. You were only eighteen." His voice was harsh.

"I didn't have much choice. You know that," I told him bitterly.

All of the pent-up anger I'd harbored toward Aiden started to roil up inside me, and I had no idea how to tamp it down.

For many months, I'd avoided him, tried to ignore how much I resented the fact that he'd never stepped up to the plate to talk about what had happened so many years ago.

"You had plenty of choices," he argued. "You had plans to go to college. But you copped out and ran away with a guy who had money while I was out on a long job. Hell, you never even hung around long enough for me to come back and say good-bye."

"You *know* what happened." I hated the fact that the devastation I'd felt back then was actually threaded through my voice.

I have to stay calm. Show no emotion.

He curled his large hand around my upper arm, which forced me to look at him. I was shocked by the surprise on his face.

Aiden had always been ruggedly handsome. His skin was always weathered, even when he was younger. And he usually had a five-o'clock shadow because the black hair grew faster than he shaved. The guy spent a lot of time outside in the elements. But with his dark hair, sexy blue eyes, and ripped, muscular body, it was a good look on him.

He was physically gorgeous.

Unfortunately, his character hadn't been as great as his appearance.

"I don't have a damn clue what happened," he said huskily. "I got back the day after you left for San Diego with a man who had a lot more to offer than I did. It didn't take long to figure out that you didn't want to live poor with a guy like me."

I hadn't given a damn about his financial

situation. I'd cared about Aiden back then, rich or not. So it pissed me off that he was making me out to be some kind of gold digger.

How could he think that I hadn't wanted him, money or not? How? I'd told him that I loved him, even though he'd never said those words back to me.

"My mother forced me into marrying Marco," I said, my heart stammering as I tried to explain something that he was already well aware of. "I wanted you to come for me, but you never did."

Dammit! I don't want to have this conversation right now. It's pointless.

His eyes searched mine. "How could she force you into it?"

Like he doesn't know how my mother got the leverage?

"If I didn't marry him, I'd no longer have a place to live."

"You could have stayed with us."

I swallowed hard as I recognized the sincerity in his voice.

Why is he acting like he doesn't understand anything that happened?

What food I'd eaten was rolling around in my stomach as reality suddenly slapped me in the face.

Is it possible that he really doesn't know?

I shook my head slowly. "I couldn't stay with you. You already had enough mouths to feed."

Aiden, Seth, and their oldest brother, Noah, had all worked to raise Jade, Brooke, and Owen, their younger siblings. And there had never been enough money. But God help me, had I known that he had wanted me to stay, I would have done anything I could to help out.

"I would have figured it out," he said gutturally.

I shook my arm out of his grasp in a panic, and then stood up. "I have to go," I told him.

My daughter was with a sitter, but that wasn't why I suddenly felt like I couldn't breathe, like I had to get some air before I passed out.

I was being bombarded by memories, and none of them were good.

I needed some time and a quiet place to get a grip. I had to deal with the fact that maybe my reality had just been turned on its head.

He doesn't know. That's why Aiden has never come and talked to me. That's why I've never heard from him.

I grabbed my purse as I struggled to breathe, my heart slamming against my chest wall so hard that I could barely make my way outside.

He doesn't know. He doesn't know.

If he did, he deserved an Academy Award for his performance.

My breathing was ragged and erratic when I ran out the door of Eli's home, and then slumped back against it in disbelief after I'd closed it behind me.

What had never been obvious to me before about Aiden came crashing down on my head.

He didn't know why I was angry.

He didn't know that I'd explained everything to him in a heartfelt letter, and then never got an answer.

He didn't know that it had destroyed me to leave with someone else.

Aiden Sinclair was *confused* about why I'd left Citrus Beach.

He had no idea that I'd been pregnant with *his* daughter when I'd gone.

CHAPTER 2
Aiden

"What in the hell was that all about?" Seth asked as he slid into the chair that Skye had just dramatically vacated. "Skye looked pissed."

I shrugged. I'd been trying for almost a year not to wonder what was going on in that beautiful blonde head of Skye Weston's, but I'd never completely succeeded. "I have no fucking idea."

I fucking hated the fact that she was still as beautiful as she had been when she was eighteen. Her expressive, big green eyes could still make me want to climb mountains to give her anything she wanted.

Hell, I should have gotten over those emotions years ago, after she'd left me for a rich guy.

The rest of my family had been momentarily distracted by Skye leaving so abruptly, but they'd gone back to their previous conversations.

I couldn't forget her departure quite as easily.

"What did she say?" Seth pressed.

"She seems to think I should know why in the hell she left. How would I know? She took off with a rich guy and left my poverty-stricken ass behind. End of story."

I'd been pretty torn up about her taking off with

a wealthy man and forgetting all about the two of us so damn easily.

Maybe we *had* been young, but Skye and I had connected in a way that I'd never experienced before and had never found again. Not even close.

When she'd come back to Citrus Beach after her mother had died, years later, I was *still* pissed off that she'd dumped me so easily. Fuck knew I'd never forgotten her, but I'd been willing to bury the hatchet since so much time had gone by. She was my sister Jade's friend.

But I'd been surprised to learn that *she* wanted nothing to do with *me,* like *I'd* done something wrong.

"Maybe she did leave a letter or something," Seth suggested uneasily.

My brother's voice was much more hesitant than usual, and since he sounded so guilty, I turned my head to look at him.

Seth and I were close. Really close. We'd grown up together with only a year between us. So I knew *that look.*

I stood and hauled him up with me so we could take it outside.

"You know something," I accused as we hit the back porch. I finally let go of his shirt. "Somebody would have needed to let Skye into the house if she'd left a note. Did you let her in? Did she leave some kind of communication or not? Tell me. No bullshit."

"What does it matter, Aiden? It's over. It was done years ago when Skye left Citrus Beach and married another guy," Seth replied as he leaned against the porch railing.

"It matters," I growled.

Seth shrugged. "Okay, maybe I *did* take the letter she left. Jesus, Aiden. You were all torn up about her leaving. The last thing you needed was a written farewell. I thought you'd be able to get over her quicker if you didn't have to read a bunch of crap from her. She left you for somebody else. What more was there to say?"

My vision was clouded with rage, and for the first time in my life, I wanted to seriously hurt one of my own brothers. "What did it say?"

"I have no idea," he admitted. "I never opened it. It wasn't addressed to me. I tossed it in the fireplace and watched it burn. Looking back, maybe it wasn't the right thing to do. But we were all working our asses off to survive. When I saw your reaction to the fact that Skye had left for San Diego with somebody else, I didn't want you to have any reminders of her around. So I took the letter before you saw it."

I rubbed the back of my neck, trying to ease the tension there. I wanted to punch my brother out for taking that letter, but I knew he'd been trying to protect me at the time. "Did she say anything?"

Seth shook his head. "No. She just said that she

was leaving for San Diego with Marco. And that she wanted to give you a letter."

Marco Marino.

A family friend of Skye's late mother.

And a bastard I'd wanted to kill when I found out he'd stolen my girl.

Marco was old enough to be Skye's father, so it wasn't difficult to figure out that his money had been a big factor in Skye's willingness to marry him. I hadn't known him personally, but I'd been damn tempted to find him in San Diego.

I'd wanted Skye back.

But I'd given up because it was obvious *she* hadn't wanted *me*.

And could I really blame her?

Back then, we'd hardly been able to survive. Noah, Seth, and I had barely made ends meet, and we'd had three younger siblings to worry about. But what I'd told Skye was true. If I'd known that her crazy, overly religious mother had threatened to turn her out, I would have found a way to keep her with me.

Seth was shifting around uncomfortably as he said, "What explanation is there for leaving a guy to marry another one with a lot of money?"

I glared at him. "I guess I'll never know, since you decided to get rid of any reasons she had."

"I'm sorry, okay? I was angry that she dumped you. And I didn't see the point in you reading about how she'd left you for somebody who had the money to support her."

I folded my arms in front of me. "You think that's why she took off? Because I couldn't take care of her?"

"What other reason could there be? Marino had nothing going for him *except* money. And even that ended up being dirty money that he made in organized crime."

My brother was right. Marco had been put in jail with all the rest of his Italian mob family before Skye had divorced him and returned to Citrus Beach to run the Weston Café. He was serving a life sentence in prison. "Do you think she knew?" I asked Seth. "Do you think she knew that he was in the mob?"

"Doubtful," he replied. "If she had, I think she'd be in jail, too."

I scraped a hand through my hair in frustration. "Why in the fuck did she do it?"

I'd spent years trying to convince myself that Skye was out to use anybody to get what she wanted. Now I didn't know what the hell to think. It had been a lot easier when I *hadn't* known she'd left a final letter. I'd been able to write her off as a woman who valued money over anything else.

Not that I'd ever forgotten her.

I still remembered what it had been like to be the first man she'd ever had, and I couldn't forget the feel of her tight, virginal body taking me inside her. I'd fallen for her hard and fast that summer, even though I'd already been a man, and she had just barely been an adult.

Maybe that was why I'd gotten so damn enraged about any other guy touching her. She'd been mine. *Only mine.* And I didn't want any other bastard looking at her, much less touching her.

"She was barely eighteen, Aiden," Seth pointed out. "And we all knew that her mother was a crazy woman. Maybe she needed a way out."

You already had enough mouths to feed.

She'd said that. Could it be that she'd at least *thought about* staying with me?

"She said her mother forced her to marry Marco," I told Seth. "That she didn't have a choice."

Seth sent me a skeptical look. "She had a choice. She could have found a way out, even though it sure as hell wouldn't have been easy. This isn't the Dark Ages. Maybe she thought it was the only way out of the loony bin back then, but it wasn't."

"Her mother really was certifiable," I said angrily.

Skye's mother had been involved in her cultlike church in San Diego for years. She'd joined when Skye's father had died of cancer. Her daughter had only been five years old.

"I didn't know Mrs. Weston very well, but she did tell me I was going to hell a couple of times," Seth answered drily.

"I think she thought *everybody* was going to hell except members of her church."

"Like Marino?" Seth questioned.

Marco Marino had been a member and a founder of the wacky religious cult. That's how Skye's mother had met him and the crime family who were supposedly upstanding members of the religious organization.

"I wish I had that goddamn letter," I said gutturally.

I wanted explanations.

I wanted to know exactly why Skye had left, and what she was thinking when she had.

I wanted to find out if she'd ever given a damn about . . . me.

Maybe it was old news, but Skye and I had never really closed our relationship. She'd just . . . left.

"If it makes you feel any better, I regret getting rid of the letter, Aiden. I really do. It was instinct."

I looked at Seth, and he *did* look pretty repentant, and regret was something I rarely saw in my brother's expression.

Yeah, I got it. Maybe I would have wanted to protect him, too, if our positions were reversed. The Sinclairs watched each other's backs. *Always.* We wouldn't have survived if we hadn't. We'd all parented each other—badly, sometimes.

But we'd done our best to make sure our siblings weren't suffering.

"Anything else you want to confess?" I asked bitterly.

"Nope. That's about the only shitty thing I did to you that I can think of right now," he said.

"Why didn't you tell me before?"

"I didn't think it mattered before. But you've never really put Skye behind you, have you? In all these years, I've never seen you serious about any other female."

"Fuck!" I grumbled.

Yeah, I'd always wanted to see Skye Weston as just a small part of my history. But ever since she'd come back to Citrus Beach with her daughter in tow, I'd wondered what in the hell had happened between the two of us. She'd been fine on the day I'd left for a two-month fishing job. We'd been planning all the things we wanted to do together in the future, and damned if I hadn't been missing her already the minute I'd left. She'd haunted me throughout that two-month job, and I'd been counting the days until I could get back to her.

But how could I have ever known that Skye would be gone when I got back home?

I finally answered Seth's question. "I don't think I ever got over her."

"Then ask her why she left," he suggested. "You don't need a letter. She's here."

Maybe so, but Skye had a history of running, just like she'd done tonight. "I tried. She seems to think she has a reason to be angry. That's why I wish I had read her letter. I have no idea what she's mad about. I didn't leave *her*. She left *me*."

"Try again. Get her someplace where she can't run away. I don't think you're ever going to move on until you get your questions answered. I wish I hadn't destroyed that letter. I wish that you would have had those answers years ago."

I nodded. "I have to know."

Seth grinned. "How long are you going to stay pissed off at me?"

I probably would have punched him out if my siblings and I hadn't learned very early on that we couldn't afford to have one less ally. Growing up, we'd been taught not to alienate each other, even if we were furious with one of our brothers or sisters. All we'd had was each other. And Seth and Noah were protective of me since I was younger than they were.

"I'm not going to get over this anytime soon," I warned him. "I was twenty-four years old. You were barely a year older. It wasn't necessary to protect me like I was a teenager."

"That instinct is never going to go away, and you know it. Jade is twenty-seven, and I still want to shake her and make sure she's marrying the right guy."

"We all like Eli," I reminded him. "Hell, he's

40

our biggest investor and advisor in Sinclair Properties."

"That doesn't mean I trust him with my sister," Seth grumbled.

It wasn't like I didn't understand exactly what my brother was telling me. We'd grown up protecting Brooke, Jade, and Owen. So it wasn't easy to let go. "She's happy."

Seth nodded. "Which is the *only reason* I'm okay with her marrying Eli Stone."

"He better make sure he keeps her that way," I added.

Seth and I understood each other perfectly . . . when it came to our younger sisters and brother.

"So a week? Two? A month? Give me some kind of guide as to when you're going to forget that I did something stupid," Seth requested.

I shot him a dirty look. We'd all done dumb things to each other at one time or another. But we were Sinclairs. We stuck together. "I'll let you know," I grumbled.

He folded his arms in front of himself stubbornly. "We are in business together. It would be kind of nice to know when I can speak to you without risking getting my head taken off."

Seth and I had moved our real-estate-developing company to what was now called the Sinclair Building in downtown Citrus Beach. It had been easier than operating from our home offices, since the company was exploding. Eli spent his weekends and other time off here in Citrus Beach, and we took all the advice we could get from our biggest investor. Eli Stone had been instrumental in helping the development company grow so quickly. Seth and I had been more than happy to let Eli invest, especially since he brought so many nonmonetary resources along with him.

"I'll be in on Monday," I informed him grimly. Seth was my best friend. Not that I'd completely forget that he'd screwed me when he'd taken that letter. But he *was* my brother.

It was Friday night, so I'd have a few days to calm down.

I dug my keys out from the pocket of my jeans and walked away without looking back at Seth.

I planned on using the next few days to figure out the mystery of why Skye thought she had a right to be angry at me.

Seth was right.

There was no way I was going to be able to look at Skye as just a small part of my history until I knew the truth.

CHAPTER 3
Skye

The next morning, I was still trying to wrap my head around the fact that Aiden didn't know that he was Maya's father.

Really, it had been so much easier to think that he knew but just didn't give a damn, and had never let any of his siblings know that they had a niece.

Jade would have said something if she'd known that Maya was her blood.

"Mommy, if I did something bad, should I tell you?" my daughter asked me in a very grave tone.

I smiled at her as I watched her devour her breakfast at the small table we'd claimed when I'd opened the café.

I had plenty of weekend help, but since most of them were college students, I still opened and closed the restaurant on the weekends, too. And since I brought Maya with me, I generally fed her breakfast here on Saturday and Sunday.

It was the beginning of spring, so only a few of the other tables were occupied. It would get busier later, but it was still early in the season. So there weren't that many tourists in this smaller coastal city.

"What did you do wrong?" I asked, trying not

to laugh at my daughter's serious expression. She'd gotten my attention by calling me *Mommy,* something she rarely did anymore unless she was in trouble.

It was hard to believe my beautiful girl could do anything all that bad. Usually, she was a quiet, thoughtful child. She was a gifted reader and writer, and she could breeze through books meant for high-school kids. Not that I let her read them all. Even though she was *capable,* Maya was very much a child and couldn't understand some of the complex emotional subjects, even if she *could* read them cover-to-cover.

She was brilliant, but her mind still thought like an eight-year-old.

My daughter looked so much like her father that my heart squeezed inside my chest. It was a miracle that nobody had ever really seemed to notice. Her dark hair and blue eyes were like copies of Aiden's.

"I really wanted to find my real dad," she said hesitantly.

My heart tripped as I looked at her sad expression. Maya had always known that Marco wasn't her biological father. I'd made it a point to tell her as soon as she was old enough to understand, since my ex-husband had treated my daughter like she didn't exist. Still, I guess I hadn't realized how curious she was about the man who was her real biological father.

"I didn't know you wanted to find him," I answered.

She nodded slowly. "I did. I just didn't want you to be sad."

I wasn't shocked that she'd picked up on my emotions. But I was surprised that I'd shown *any* reaction. I'd pretty much learned to bury most of my feelings.

"So what did you do, then? Tell me."

"I got my DNA tested. I have an aunt right here in Citrus Beach. Somebody matched. She wrote to me and told me she lives here, and that I have a bunch of other aunts and uncles, too. But I didn't write back to her because I had to cancel my membership. I didn't have money to extend it."

Jade? She'd matched with Jade?

It made sense, since the DNA site was the way Jade had found her long-lost family on the East Coast, and had subsequently gotten her siblings their share of the enormous inheritance they were entitled to.

But . . . "How did you ever manage to get the tests done? You have to be eighteen, right?" I asked Maya nervously.

She put her fork on her empty plate and reached for her milk before she answered. "That's what I did wrong," she said. "I used my credit card to pay for the DNA test. And I lied about my age."

My daughter didn't *really* have a credit card. She

45

had a prepaid card that I made sure was always in her backpack. Maya was intelligent enough to understand that it was only for emergencies.

Now that she was almost done with third grade, she *definitely* knew she wasn't to use it unless she had to. "That's for emergencies," I told her. "You know that."

She nodded. "I know. It was wrong. But I really wanted to know who my dad was."

I lifted a brow. "And you couldn't have just asked me?"

Her eyes welled up with tears, which nearly broke me. Maya hadn't exactly had a happy childhood so far, and that was entirely my fault for marrying someone like Marco.

"I wanted to ask, but I don't think you like him, whoever he is. Like I said, you always looked sad when I mentioned my real dad. And I don't want you to be sad again. We've been sad a lot. And we're pretty happy now."

My own tears threatened to fall, but I blinked them back because of my ingrained instinct to remain stoic. Even though I'd tried to shield Maya from the scandal of Marco and his family going to jail, and the long trial that put him there, she'd been exposed to ridicule and the stress I'd tried so hard to hide.

The Marino family had been well known in San Diego. And she hadn't been spared from the gossip.

It had been a relief when I'd been able to move away from the city, back to Citrus Beach, where most people wouldn't even ask her about her stepfamily.

She'd told me that third grade in Citrus Beach was her best year ever.

And I'd hoped she could finally live a normal life.

But she'd obviously been hiding her questions.

"We're *very happy* now," I reassured her. "I'm disappointed that you used your card. But I understand why you did. Just don't do it again, okay?"

She put down her empty glass and shook her head. "I won't. I swear."

Maya had been through enough. I wasn't going to punish her for being curious. Especially since I hadn't exactly been forthcoming with her in the first place.

But how could I tell her that her father lived right here in town, yet he didn't really communicate with her?

That was a lot to put on an eight-year-old, but I'd *had* to come back to Citrus Beach. I needed to make a go of the café so that Maya could have a decent life. I hadn't been able to go to college, and making the restaurant fly was the only way I could actually earn a decent living.

"I'm so sorry all this has been so hard for you," I told her earnestly.

She shrugged. "I'm okay. I have you. I don't really need a dad."

Maybe she didn't *need* one, but she was entitled to know who he was. I'd just never wanted her to be disappointed.

I have to tell Aiden the truth.

If he truly didn't know that Maya was his daughter, then he had a right to know, too.

What if he really had never gotten my letter explaining that I was pregnant, and I didn't know what to do?

When I'd told my mother that I was pregnant with Aiden Sinclair's child, she'd pretty much disowned me. The only option she'd given me was to marry a man from her church, a guy old enough to be my father.

It was either that, or I'd end up homeless *and* pregnant.

Maybe I'd been young and stupid, but I had loved Maya from the moment I'd discovered that she existed. I'd wanted her to be safe.

I'd left with Marco, but I'd never given up hope that Aiden would come for me.

And when he didn't, I'd been destroyed.

My daughter had been the only thing I'd lived for once I'd realized that Aiden wasn't going to come and get us.

"I'll tell you about him soon, okay?" I told my daughter. "I have a few things I have to do first."

Maya nodded her dark head. "Do you think he

lives here, too? If I have an aunt here, do you think they live in the same town? I saw another person on the site who was related, but he was only a part uncle. I didn't write to him, though."

Evan? It had to have been Evan Sinclair, the oldest Sinclair brother on the East Coast and Jade's half brother.

I let out a sigh of relief that Maya hadn't contacted *him*. Jade adored her half brother, but I'd always found him to be pretty intimidating. The East Coast Sinclairs had grown up filthy rich, unlike Jade and all her siblings. But taking a DNA test had given Jade a second family when she'd matched with Evan—and the fortune that went with being related to the wealthy Sinclair family that originated from Boston. Maybe Jade's father *had* been a bully bigamist, but at least he'd been a very rich one.

I had to at least like Evan because he'd been fair about distributing the wealth to all of his half-siblings—once he'd learned of their existence—here in California.

I grabbed my mug and took a large gulp of my coffee before I asked, "How did you get into that site, anyway? You should be blocked."

My daughter had her own tablet, but there were only certain places she could access.

Maya looked sheepish. "I had to kind of borrow your laptop."

"Kind of?" I said disapprovingly.

She looked down at her empty plate. "Okay, I *did* borrow it. A couple of times. Lena falls asleep on the couch sometimes when you're working late."

Lena was one of Maya's college-aged babysitters.

Rather than being angry, I felt a pang of guilt that my daughter had to spend so damn much time with babysitters. "You're shut down on my computer, Sugar Bug," I warned her.

"Mom, I'm too old to be called that nickname. And I already deleted my membership. I won't use your computer again. I already promised I wouldn't."

I believed her. Maya was a curious kid, but she'd never been deliberately disobedient. In fact, she'd been easy to raise so far. She was kind, considerate, loving, and the sort of child all mothers everywhere wanted to have. "It doesn't matter how old you get, you'll always be my Sugar Bug," I said fondly. "And yes, your father *does* live here."

Her eyes lit up, and I wanted to kick myself. Maybe I shouldn't have said anything until I talked to Aiden.

But now that I was committed to talking to him about Maya, I was hoping he'd want to know her.

I'd always known I was at least going to have to tell Jade that she had a niece. She was my best friend. I'd just never figured out how to tell her without revealing that Aiden didn't care if he had a child or not.

But maybe that's not true. Maybe he really never knew.

Now I was almost sure that was the case. And it was a scary thought.

What if he wants his daughter? What if he tries to take her away from me?

Since I couldn't even cope with the thought that Maya could go anywhere but home with me, I pushed the negative voices out of my head.

"Will I be able to meet him?" Maya asked hopefully.

"We'll see. I have to talk to him first." I didn't want to tell her that her dad might not even know that he'd fathered a daughter.

Or that her mother had been so damn hurt by her father that I might have unknowingly kept her existence from him for over nine long years.

CHAPTER 4
Skye

Later that morning, I forced myself to ring the doorbell at Aiden's magnificent beachfront home before I lost my nerve.

All of the inevitable questions had been racing through my brain since I'd left Maya with Jade and then made my way down the beach to talk to Aiden.

What if he doesn't believe me?

What if he doesn't want to see Maya once he knows?

What if he wants to take my daughter away from me?

What if . . .

What if . . .

What if . . .

Maya deserved the chance to have a father, if Aiden was willing, but that didn't mean I was happy about having to confront him with the truth.

My daughter had been through so damn much, and all I wanted to do was protect her, so it went against my instincts to take a chance on the fact that she might be disappointed.

I distinctly remembered Aiden once telling

52

me that he didn't really want any children of his own, since he'd already brought up his siblings.

I had to wonder if he still thought that way, now that he had the resources to have as many kids as he wanted.

I jumped when the door suddenly flew open and Aiden stood in front of me with a scowl on his face.

"We need to talk," I said in a breathless voice before he could get out a single word. "Please."

My heart skipped a beat as he continued to scrutinize me carefully before opening the door wider so I could come in.

The foyer was gorgeous, vaulted ceilings giving the space elegance and grandeur. It was a beautiful home on the beach, but I didn't give the mansion's appearance much more thought.

I was too nervous, and too rattled by seeing Aiden.

He looked approachable in a pair of jeans and a T-shirt, his hair apparently still damp from a shower.

"Come in," he rumbled as he headed for a large chef's kitchen. "You want coffee?"

I followed him. "No, thanks. I had plenty at the restaurant this morning."

I watched as he made himself a cup. I wasn't surprised that Aiden was pretty much at home in the kitchen. After all, he'd had to cook for his siblings many times.

"Sit," he demanded as he nodded at the small kitchen table.

I sat, never thinking about the fact that I was obeying his orders. Honestly, I needed to plant my ass in a chair before I fell down.

Aiden pulled out another chair and sat across from me.

"I was going to go looking for you shortly, so I'm glad you're here," he told me, and then took a slug of his coffee.

I fidgeted with the purse I'd laid on the table, unable to look at him as I spoke. "Is it really true that you don't know why I left nine years ago?"

"I have no damn clue," he answered gruffly. "But after you ran out last night, Seth told me you left a letter at the house. Want to tell me what it said?"

I finally looked at him in surprise. "You didn't read it?"

"Never got a chance to," he confessed. "Seth burned it."

I listened while Aiden explained what had happened with his brother, and how he ended up never knowing all the things I told him in that missive.

"All I knew was that you'd taken off with a rich guy, a man who had a lot more to offer you than I did," he concluded.

"Marco had nothing to offer me *except* money," I explained. "But that's not why I had to go."

He folded his muscular arms across his chest and leaned back in his chair. "Then explain to me why you had to go, if you didn't care about money."

"I told you. I would have had no place to live. I either had to go with Marco or end up on the streets."

"I would have helped you, Skye. I think you knew I would."

A big part of me *had* known that Aiden would move heaven and earth just to make sure I was safe. But I'd had no idea how he would have felt if he'd known that I was pregnant. I'd been hoping he'd want to protect his child, too, which was why I'd written that letter.

"It's over," I said, hating the fact that those two words were filled with pain. "We have to move on."

In hindsight, I wished I *had* found a way to wait until Aiden had gotten home, but I couldn't change the past. I'd been stupid, young, and terrified. I regretted the fact that Maya had been deprived of family. All she'd ever had was me.

"Then by all means, let's move on," Aiden agreed. "Why are you here now? Are you looking to reconnect now that I have money?"

My anger flared, but I pushed it back down. Maybe I deserved that slam, since he was under the impression that I'd left him for more money-green pastures. "I don't really want anything from you, but I have to tell you some things I think you need to know."

"Such as?"

"I wanted to stay here," I explained. "When my mother insisted that I go to San Diego and marry Marco, I didn't want to do it. We fought pretty hard the day before you came back. We barely spoke after I married."

"What about her grandchild?" Aiden questioned.

I shook my head sadly. "She didn't care about Maya. My mother wasn't exactly the grandmotherly type. She was sick in the head, Aiden. You know she was always crazy, but she was also brainwashed by the crazy church she attended in San Diego."

"I'm sure she thought you were better off with him than me," Aiden drawled.

"Marco's parents were founding members of that church. That's all she cared about. She thought I'd be lucky to have him. She never realized that she was part of a cult. Granted, they didn't live in a commune, but that religious group had a hold on her, regardless."

"How did you even meet your ex-husband?" he asked roughly. "I remember that you never went to that church once you got old enough to tell your mother that you didn't want to go."

"When I was seventeen, I *did* go with my mom a couple of times. I wanted to make her happy.

But it only lasted for a short time. I didn't like being there. The whole thing gave me the creeps. And so did Marco. He saw me there and decided he wanted me to be his wife. I think he wanted that all the more after I'd flatly refused to marry him. I wasn't even out of high school yet when he asked my mother if he could marry me."

"So you said no?"

I nodded. "And I refused to go to any events there ever again."

"Then why in the hell did you give in later?" he asked in an angry tone.

I shrugged. "My circumstances had changed. I was desperate, Aiden."

"And was your mother right?" he pressed. "Were you lucky to have him? Were you happy?"

"No," I said in a voice that was little more than a whisper. "The only happy part of my marriage was my daughter. Maya was everything to me. She still is."

"What in the hell did the letter say? What did you want to tell me? Did you want me to come and find you?"

"I did," I admitted. "I asked you to come find me if you really loved me. To get me out of marrying a man I didn't love."

"But you never heard from me because I never read that letter," he concluded. "I was left to assume that you wanted to be with somebody else because he had more money than I did."

"I never wanted you to think that," I told him adamantly. "Did I really seem like that kind of woman?"

Maybe I could understand why he had felt that way, but it still hurt.

"I had no idea what to think," he said. "I still don't. But if I had known that you didn't want to be with Marino, I sure as hell would have found you."

"I didn't know that," I said in a tremulous voice. "I thought you'd just trashed the letter after you'd read it, and you didn't think about me anymore."

I flinched as Aiden's fist came down on the table. Hard.

"You knew damn well that I was crazy about you," he snapped. "Did you really think I wouldn't have responded to a cry for help from you?"

I'd been so damn hurt that I'd thought exactly that. When Aiden hadn't shown up to take me away, I'd given up all hope of being happy. All I'd focused on was my daughter, and survival.

But honestly, now that I was older, I probably *should* have wondered why a man like Aiden had just chucked me out of his life without another thought. "Just like you, I didn't know what to think," I said quietly. "I was scared."

"So where in the hell do we go from here?" he grumbled. "We didn't even have enough faith in each other to go and find out the truth."

"I'm not here to get you back. I know you don't believe me, and I don't blame you for that. Really, we hardly knew each other. We only went out for a couple of months."

The time for me and Aiden had passed a long time ago.

"So you just wanted to close this chapter of our life?"

"Not exactly." I tried to swallow the lump in my throat. "There's another reason why I was really scared of becoming homeless. If it had just been me, I would have done it. But it *wasn't* just me."

He gave me an assessing look, one that seemed to be able to see my soul. "Who else was there?" he asked, sounding confused.

I took a deep breath. "I was pregnant, Aiden. I think I conceived the night before you left for your long fishing job. Maya isn't Marco's child. She's yours. My little girl is *your daughter*."

CHAPTER 5
Skye

The silence in Aiden's enormous home was deafening.

He didn't speak.

He didn't react.

He didn't move.

But I could see the shock and horror in his expression.

That long, stretched-out period with no words spoken between us was the instant I truly realized that Aiden had *never* known the truth. He really *had* thought I'd left him for money without a qualm.

Maybe I'd understood that with my head since last night, but I hadn't known it in my heart . . . until now.

It was hard to change nine years of disappointment and sadness over the fact that he hadn't wanted Maya in his life, but the truth had just slapped me in the face.

He hadn't not wanted her.

He hadn't not cared.

And he sure as hell would have been there for both of us if he'd known.

He just . . . hadn't had a clue.

I was flooded with regret, an emotion I was perfectly familiar with. Regret and guilt seemed to be the two feelings I could never banish. They lived with me like the only items of clothing I owned, clinging to my skin.

It's better that he didn't know.

Considering the mess I'd gotten myself into with the Marino family, Aiden *not knowing* had probably saved his life. But those thoughts were cold comfort as I stared at the face of a man who looked completely devastated.

"I'm sorry," I said softly, finally breaking the silence between us. "I didn't know that you never got the letter."

His expression was thunderous as he stared back at me, his blue eyes darker in his anger. "So what, Skye?" he growled. "You thought I had just ignored the fact that I supposedly have a daughter? That I could go on living my life not knowing how she was, or how she was doing without a father? Jesus Christ! You never really knew me at all, did you? What kind of guy does that?"

Don't cry. Don't let him see that you have emotions. Don't let him see your weaknesses.

I'd been so well trained by the years I'd spent with Marco that my survival instincts took over.

My heart was breaking.

But I'd be damned if anybody would ever know it.

My daughter's safety had always depended on the way I handled *the family*.

"I don't think either one of us really knew each other," I said flatly. "You thought I'd leave for the money, and I was under the impression that you knew about Maya but didn't want to be part of her life."

"I would have wanted to be part of her life. For fuck's sake, I raised my siblings, sacrificed whatever I had to in order to give them a better life. Did you really think I'd feel any differently about my own daughter?"

Unable to look at his furious expression anymore, I turned my eyes to the surface of the table.

"I was young, alone, and pregnant, Aiden. Do you really think I had a lot of rational thoughts? I wanted my baby to be safe. That's all I was thinking about."

"Why in the hell didn't you contact me again before you married the mob?" His voice was raw. "Why didn't you check to make sure I got your letter, and that I knew that the baby was mine?"

I shrugged. "Why didn't you find out for sure why I'd left with Marco?"

"It seemed pretty damn obvious," he snapped.

"As obvious as your rejection appeared to be. Look, I'm not saying I did the right thing," I explained. "But it seemed like the only solution for me at the time."

Feeling restless, I stood up. Aiden rose from his seat, too.

"You're not leaving until I have answers," he said in a slightly calmer voice. "We could rehash all the details over and over again, but it isn't going to change the fact that I have a daughter I've never gotten to know and never knew existed. Your days of running away from everything are over."

I flinched at the insult, but maybe he was right. When I was eighteen, I *had* run away. It was only as an adult that I learned to face things head-on.

"I wasn't planning on going anywhere. If I hadn't wanted you to know, I wouldn't be here right now."

Aiden scraped a hand through his hair in apparent frustration. "Was he good to her? Did he treat her like a daughter?"

I wasn't even going to pretend I didn't understand what he was asking. If the roles were reversed, I'd want to know the same thing. "Marco never took to Maya. He was never abusive to her physically. He just pretended like she really didn't exist."

I'd been more than willing to take any punishment my ex-husband had dealt out so he didn't turn his malevolence toward my daughter.

"He knew you were pregnant?"

I nodded. "He used the pregnancy as a way of getting me to marry him. I would have never done it if he hadn't known and understood that my child was my priority. But after we were married, he completely ignored her, and I kept Maya away from him as much as possible."

"So the bastard resented her?"

"He did," I answered honestly. "But maybe that was for the best considering how everything turned out in the end."

There had been far too many misunderstandings, and I was determined to be as up front as possible with Aiden.

"Did you know what he was when you married him? Did you know that the whole Marino family was dirty?"

"No," I said quickly. "Do you really think I would have put our child into that situation if I had known?"

He glared at me. "I don't know what to think anymore, Skye. All I know is that I want my daughter. I've already missed a hell of a lot of things in her life. Now that I'm well able to support her, she might be better off with me."

Don't cry. Don't cry.

"I'm her mother. She belongs with *me*. She doesn't even know you yet, Aiden. But I'm not going to try to keep her from you. She can see you whenever you want."

"Are you fucking kidding me?" he snarled. "I've missed over eight years of her life. I want her full time. I want to make up for those years that I lost. I want to be the father she's obviously never had, and that she deserves."

"I can't give you that," I refused. "I'm the only stable thing Maya has ever known."

And I love her so much that she's my entire life.

My stomach was rolling with fear, but I kept myself together. I had to.

"Then I'll be another constant in her life," he stated like it was a vow. "And she'll have plenty of family here."

My heart squeezed. Real family was something Maya craved. "She's my daughter. I'm not giving her up. You can get to know her without taking her away from me."

"I'll want a paternity test," he said ruthlessly. "But I'm not waiting for the results to be in her life. Since you were a virgin, I'm pretty doubtful that I'm not her biological father. And I'm going to do a hell of a lot more than *get to know her*. I'm going to be her dad like I always should have been."

"So we're going to end up fighting over her?" I asked, my heart broken by the thought that Maya could become caught in the middle.

"No," he said stonily. "No fights. It sounds like she's had enough upheaval. You're both coming to live with me. And then after Jade leaves, and her wedding is over, we're getting married."

I shook my head instantly. "No."

Aiden moved forward like a predator, pinning

me against the counter of the breakfast bar. "Do you have a better solution?"

I closed my eyes, trying to will away the visceral reaction I'd always had when my body made contact with Aiden's.

I didn't want it.

I didn't want to feel it.

I didn't want to want him. And I shouldn't after all these years.

He took my chin and tipped it up. "Look at me," he commanded.

I opened my eyes, and I met the most determined stare I'd ever encountered.

Aiden wanted his daughter. And I knew how stubborn he could be.

"Marriage is never a good solution to anything," I said, my voice wavering slightly. "I don't want to get married again. Ever."

"Even if it means you could give your daughter everything? I'm not a poor man anymore, Skye. I could give Maya the world."

I felt a twinge of guilt. "Money doesn't make people happy. I know that from personal experience."

"I'd give her the love of a real family, of a real father," he coerced.

"She can have that without us having to get married. This is the twenty-first century, Aiden. Parents don't have to be married. We can work this out."

"I'm not willing to settle for occasional visits, Skye. Or us shifting our daughter back and forth. If I'm pressed, I *will* fight for her. And I have an endless amount of money to make sure I win."

And I don't have the funds to fight him.

I was besieged by panic when I said, "We'll come live with you for a while. Give you the chance to get to know each other."

He was still holding my chin up so he could see my eyes, and I hated it. I didn't want to be vulnerable to this man, and I knew I couldn't completely hide my fear of losing Maya.

I stared back at him, unwilling to give in, but I was definitely weakening.

If Aiden could really be the father Maya never had, if he could really love her, I didn't want to take that away from her. But I couldn't stand the thought of losing her, either.

"That would be a start," Aiden agreed grudgingly. "I'll send a crew to help you move tomorrow morning. All you'll really need is your personal stuff."

"I can't just move in one day," I protested.

"There isn't much I can't make happen anymore, Skye. And I want to spend time with Maya. I think I've waited long enough."

The rougher and rawer tone of his voice touched me like his anger hadn't. There was a longing in his words that made my chest ache.

It was hard to reconcile the billionaire that

Aiden was now with the struggling blue-collar man he'd been when he was younger.

Now he was an enigma I truly didn't know.

But my body still reacted, just the same as it had all those years ago, to his close proximity to me.

I squirmed until I got my freedom, and put several feet of distance between us.

"Fine," I told him breathlessly. "We'll be here in the morning."

"I say we tell Maya that there was a misunderstanding, and that I never knew she was my daughter. It's pretty much the truth."

I lifted a brow. "And you think that's really going to fly? You don't know your daughter yet. She's going to ask questions. Plenty of them. She's gifted with language—writing and reading. And she's more mature than most kids."

"Then we'll answer them as honestly as possible. We'll let her know that she's important, and that you wanted her to be safe."

I was relieved and slightly touched that he wasn't going to try to blame me for what happened. At least not to my daughter's face.

"She knows that I made some mistakes," I explained. "I've always been as honest as I could with her. She was smart enough to know that being in the Marino family wasn't normal."

"Then let's give her normal, Skye," he rumbled.

God, I wanted that for my daughter so badly that

the ache I'd been feeling turned into a physical pain in my stomach. My daughter had always been way too serious for her age. Even though I'd tried to give her all the love I had, she'd still been in a bad atmosphere for way too long. A place where nobody had even acknowledged her existence except me.

I nodded as I said, "We'll be here in the morning."

I didn't want my daughter part time. I was going to have to give Aiden a chance to know her, but I wanted to be with her, too. So if that meant I had to move into Aiden's home, I'd do it.

It wasn't like I was going to miss our tiny apartment. It was always clean, but it was more than a little drab, no matter what I tried to do to make it brighter.

"I'll pick you up around nine," he insisted. "I'll send a truck with a crew to get your stuff around eight thirty."

"I wish I knew if we were doing the right thing," I mused aloud before I could censor my words.

"She'll be fine, Skye. I'll make sure she's always okay," he affirmed.

I searched his eyes, and found a committed determination that actually helped me relax.

His comments made me feel safe.

For so long, I'd been the only one who had been there for Maya no matter what. There was some kind of relief in knowing I wasn't all alone in those goals anymore.

"What are we going to tell your family?" I asked hesitantly.

"The truth," he drawled. "I think they'll all be ecstatic about having Maya in the family. It's not like the Sinclairs are exactly hesitant to have more relatives."

I shot him a small smile because I knew the Sinclair family had grown significantly over the last few years. It had exploded with growth once Aiden and his siblings had discovered that they had a slew of half-siblings and cousins on the East Coast.

I strode to the table and picked up my purse. "I need to go. Maya is with a sitter."

He grabbed me by the upper arm to stop me. "You work a lot. You look exhausted, Skye. Is that really what you want? Is the Weston Café what you really want?"

I easily shrugged out of his hold on me. "Does it matter? It's my way of supporting Maya."

It had been a hell of a long time since anybody had asked me what I wanted, and I wasn't quite sure how to answer him. The café was an icon in Citrus Beach, but working long hours there, and spending so much time away from Maya, had never been my choice.

I did it to survive.

"If you're marrying me, your choices will become unlimited," he said huskily.

"It's my security," I tried to explain. "It brings in some income."

"I plan to take my daughter to see the world," he warned. "If you want to be with her, you'll need to find a manager, and more staff. Honestly, that dinosaur could use a serious makeover. The painting made it look better, but the building is old. It must need repairs. Maybe you need to think about turning it into something you can love by doing a complete remodel. I'd invest in you and your ideas. But you aren't going to need to be involved in the day-to-day stuff."

"I've always wanted it to be so much more," I confessed. "But I didn't have the funds to sink into making the place something different."

He shrugged. "Now you do, if that's what you want."

My heart tripped at the possibility that I could really transform the café into a success instead of a restaurant where I could barely eke out a living.

I eyed him with curiosity. "Why would you want to do that?"

"You're the mother of my child, Skye. I want you to be happy. You're going to be my wife."

I balked. "I'm still not sure about the marriage part of the deal."

"I'm *not over* wanting that," he warned. "In fact, the idea keeps sounding better and better. You said you never wanted to marry again, and I had no plans to get hitched, either. So there's no reason why we can't become a family for our daughter."

"We don't even like each other anymore," I said desperately.

He shrugged. "Then we learn to put our differences aside to raise our daughter together."

What about friendship?

What about mutual respect?

What about love?

What about . . . sex?

I shuddered. I hadn't really wanted the last one on my mental list for a long time. But Aiden was bound to want to screw a woman eventually. He'd always had an insatiable sexual appetite.

"I'm not agreeing to marry you." I was putting my foot down. "Let's just give Maya a chance to get to know you right now."

"Let's do both," he said with a small grin.

"You're exasperatingly stubborn," I accused.

"I am when I want to take care of what's mine," he said in a dangerous tone.

My heart started to gallop as I turned to leave. "We'll see you tomorrow."

I wasn't going to win the argument, so I'd just try to convince him *after* we'd moved in together that marriage wasn't the answer.

It never was.

CHAPTER 6
Aiden

"Turns out, I fathered a child," I announced bluntly to my siblings later that night. "I have a daughter. She's eight years old."

I'd called a family meeting, and my brother and sisters had turned up without asking many questions. Noah, Jade, and Brooke had all arrived right on time.

I'd had very little doubt that all of them would be curious, since we'd never actually *had* a family meeting.

The only one *not* currently staring at me like I'd grown multiple heads was Seth. He *hadn't* been invited because I really, really wanted to hurt him right now. There was no way he would have been safe if we were in the same room.

Owen, my youngest sibling, hadn't come into town yet for Jade's wedding, so he'd find out a little later, too.

"How is that possible?" Noah asked calmly, because Noah was always the most levelheaded, as our eldest sibling.

I raised an eyebrow. "You're the one who told me how women got pregnant, when we were younger."

Noah had even gone so far as to show us how to use a condom with a banana once. And I *had* used a rubber with Skye. My guess was that we were one of a small handful of failures.

My eldest sibling had been there for all of our questions growing up. It was strange that he'd seemed so grown up when he was only a few years older than I was.

"You know that's not what I meant," Noah grumbled.

My family was still gaping at me from their seats in my family room. "I dated Skye Weston for a while, right after she graduated from high school. She was pregnant with my child when she moved to San Diego and married Marco Marino. I never knew. We had a miscommunication and she thought I blew her off."

"Maya is your child?" Jade asked incredulously.

I nodded.

"Oh, my God," she said. "Somebody wrote to me from the DNA site. They matched me as the child's aunt. But I never knew it was somebody so close, or so young. I know she's gifted, but her message sounded like somebody older, and children usually can't send in their DNA to be analyzed."

I grinned. "She must take after me. She's pretty damn smart. And she obviously knows how to break the rules. Why didn't you say something about a match on the site?"

It was always strange when we didn't know everything about our sisters. Noah, Seth, and I certainly knew how to get into their business. We'd made it our personal mission to screen every man they dated.

Jade frowned. "I never heard from her again after one communication, and I had no idea who she was. Eli was trying to do some investigating to figure out which one of you fathered a child. I didn't want to spill the beans without any information. I knew it would bother all of you until we figured it out. I was going to tell you before the wedding. But I guess the mystery is solved. I wonder why Skye never told me."

I knew it probably pained Jade that her best friend had never shared her secret. "Probably because she assumed that I knew and just didn't give a damn."

"Can I meet her?" Brooke, Jade's twin, asked excitedly.

"After I do," I said drily. "I still can't believe I have a daughter who I don't know."

I'd only had a matter of hours to get used to the fact that I was a father. I was pretty sure it was going to take a hell of a lot longer to be comfortable with it.

"You'll love her," Jade said warmly. "Maya is special. Gifted, so she can be a challenge. She'll ask a million questions. But she has an enormous heart."

Jade was gifted, too. So I knew my sister could relate to my daughter. Jade had gotten her doctorate in record time, and she was a genius in her field of wildlife genetics.

"I'm just a blue-collar guy," I said in a hesitant tone that I didn't even recognize.

I wondered how Maya would feel if I couldn't so much as help her with her homework someday.

I'd always loved to read, and I preferred it to television. But I hadn't ever had enough time to read everything I wanted until recently.

Keeping the Sinclair family afloat had been an all-consuming task when we'd had limited funds. Noah, Seth, and I had spent almost every waking hour working.

Jade smiled. "That isn't going to matter to her."

"I think I can give her a hell of a lot better life than she had with the mob family," I said huskily.

At least I would never treat her like she didn't exist.

"You can give her an *amazing life,*" Brooke said. "Aiden, you were *always* there for us. It isn't like you don't know how to raise a kid and give them a ton of love. She's not going to care about your education level."

I leaned back in my recliner. "I hope you're right, because someday she'll be way smarter than I am. I'd like to give her all the education she wants. But at least I have a lot of money now. I can give her everything she needs."

"Are you going to share custody with Skye?" Noah questioned, his expression still puzzled.

"They'll both be living here as of tomorrow morning," I announced. "I want to get to know my daughter. I've already missed so much of her life. I don't want her part time, and I think she deserves better than being shifted back and forth."

Brooke clapped. "So you're getting back together with Skye?"

"No," I said flatly. "Not exactly. But since she doesn't want to be without her daughter, they're both coming to live with me. We'll get married eventually."

"Are you serious?" Noah asked roughly. "You don't have to get married to parent a child together."

My eldest brother was sounding a lot like Skye. "Maybe not. But it's happening anyway. The only other options are to share custody, or fight for primary custody. After all that Maya has been through, I don't want that to happen."

And I sure as hell couldn't imagine Skye and me living in the same household while we were dating other people.

That *was not* happening.

"You're pissed off at Skye. I can tell," Jade observed.

"How can I not be? She never told me that she'd had my child. She just ran off and married somebody else."

77

Jade spoke up. "There's more to the story. There has to be. I've been friends with her since grade school. She'd never do that. And you said it was a misunderstanding. That she thought you knew."

"I was on a long fishing job. Apparently her mother flipped out when she found out Skye was pregnant, and told her she had to marry Marino. I hadn't gotten back yet, so she left a letter."

"What happened to the letter?" Noah asked.

"Seth decided to destroy it," I told him. "He thought it would be better if I didn't read it, since Skye had left with another man. He didn't know she was pregnant with my kid."

Understanding dawned on Noah's face. "Ahhh . . . so that explains why he's not here."

"I want to hurt him," I answered honestly. "He literally robbed me of eight years of my child's life."

"His intentions were probably good," Noah mused.

"I don't give a shit about his motivations right now."

I was livid with Seth. Now that I knew that Skye had been pregnant with my child, the thought of my brother destroying a critical communication from her royally pissed me off.

"It will blow over," Noah said confidently.

"Don't hold your breath," I warned him.

"Please don't punish Skye," Jade pleaded.

"There's a lot we don't know about what happened with her marriage, but I know it wasn't good. Maybe Maya wasn't in the best of situations, but I *can* guarantee you Skye loves her daughter and did the best she could to keep her safe."

"Let's get back to the marriage part of this," Noah said as he folded his arms across his chest. "Marrying her is not a good idea. If you two hate each other, what kind of atmosphere is that for Maya?"

"I don't exactly hate her," I confessed. "I'm just angry right now."

If I'd been thinking logically—which I wasn't—I probably wouldn't have been such a bastard to Skye this morning. Truth was, my dick still coveted her. I never had been able to control the attraction between the two of us. But finding out that she'd birthed a kid I'd never known about had sent me over the edge. Especially since I'd never been able to keep myself in check around her.

Skye Weston brought out the best *and* the worst of me because she made me as irrational as hell. She always had.

It fucking hurt that she had actually thought I wouldn't give a damn about my own daughter.

I might be insanely attracted to Skye, but I realized that she'd never really known me all that well at all.

"She was only eighteen, Aiden," Jade reminded me. "Give her a break. She honestly didn't have very many options. Her mother was loony tunes, and it sounds like Skye had nowhere to go. I can't imagine having to deal with that when I was eighteen. The only thing I worried about was starting college at that age. I don't think I was mature enough to handle having a child."

I shifted uncomfortably because I knew Jade was probably right. Skye had been so damn young when she'd gotten pregnant, and I had to shoulder a lot of the blame. I had been quite a few years older than her. "If she just would have come back and told me in person."

"She didn't because she thought you knew and were ignoring the whole situation," Brooke said. "You knew each other for what? A few months?"

"She was just Jade's friend. Obviously I'd known her for longer than that."

Brooke let out an exasperated sigh. "But you saw her as a kid before you dated her. It's not the same thing."

Maybe my sisters were correct. And maybe I should have kept my dick in my pants since Skye *had been* young. But there had been no chance of that once I'd gotten to know her.

There had been no resisting Skye. She'd made me crazy.

"You don't have to decide your whole future today," Noah said. "You just found out that you have a child. Get to know her. It's going to be a big adjustment."

My sisters both nodded their agreement.

"I still can't believe that Maya is my niece," Jade said happily. "But it makes so much sense now. She looks so much like you, Aiden. I'm not sure why I never suspected it before. And the timing matches up."

"I'm getting a paternity test," I shared.

"As you should," Noah agreed.

"For some reason, I feel it in my gut that Skye is telling the truth." There was really no reason for her to lie about it. She sure as hell didn't act like she was itching to get the two of us back together.

In fact, she'd been pretty damn adamant about not getting married again.

"She'd never lie about it," Jade said firmly.

"Is she really moving here tomorrow morning? That's fast," Brooke said. "How are they going to get everything together to move?"

I grinned at her. "That's one of the perks of having so much money that I don't have to think about the details. The moving crews are already arranged."

"Which room are you giving Maya?" Jade asked.

I hadn't thought about the sleeping arrangements. "I'm not sure. I don't really have a room decorated for an eight-year-old. Damn! I guess I should have thought about that." We'd had a girly room in the house for my sisters when they were kids, and it had never entered my head to do the same for my daughter.

This father thing was going to take some getting used to. Brooke and Jade hadn't been that young in a long time.

"I know what she likes," Jade said as she stood. "I think it's time to go shopping. The mall will still be open."

My ass got out of the recliner instantly. The last thing I wanted was for Maya to not feel like she was at home here.

"I'm coming, too," Brooke said as she hopped up.

"I want to meet my niece, but I can do without the shopping expedition," Noah said as he rose to his feet. "But I'd like it if you could get her something from me. I'll give you the money."

Brooke made a face at Noah. "I'll get her something from you. I don't need the money to do that for you."

Noah nodded. "I'll owe you."

We all looked at my eldest brother.

I knew exactly what my sisters were thinking.

What Noah had given *all of us* was something we'd *never* be able to pay back. He'd kept us together as a family, and sacrificed his own life in the process. He'd been a mother, a father, and an older brother all at the same time. And he'd fought to retain custody of us all because he was the only legal adult among us when my mother had died.

But he'd never, ever complained about giving up his life for his family.

In reality, we owed Noah, and always would.

"I have some stuff I need to do in the office," Noah explained as he headed for the door.

"It's Saturday night," Brooke called out after him.

The door closed solidly without a reply from my eldest brother.

"He works too much," Jade said with a sigh.

"He always has," Brooke agreed. "What good is having all that money when he never seems to spend any of it? He needs a vacation. Maybe we should give him one for Christmas or his birthday."

Somehow, I couldn't see Noah relaxing with a cocktail on a beach somewhere, but I didn't want to burst my sisters' bubble. "I'd pitch in for that."

My twin sisters both smiled at me. "Right now, we need to take care of what you need for tomorrow," Brooke said.

I put an arm around each of them. "Lead the way."

They both chattered as they headed for the door.

It was moments like this that made me grateful for the fact that I had a really large family.

I had to work hard to push the thought that Skye had never had *anyone* out of my mind.

She'd been little more than a girl trying desperately to hang on to her child.

Our child.

That line of thought haunted me for the rest of the night.

CHAPTER 7
Skye

"I'm so happy that you're my dad," Maya told Aiden with an enormous smile as we tucked her into the bed in her new room.

I'd hung back a little as Aiden sat on the edge of the bed. I knew he needed his time with his daughter, and I'd already had over eight years with her. I wanted him to get Maya's undivided attention.

Our move-in day had gone surprisingly well. Aiden had hired people to take care of everything, and all I'd needed to do was put our personal things away.

My daughter had been thrilled when she saw her new room, and it had touched me that Aiden had obviously gotten someone to make a personal space that made my daughter squeal with delight. Not to mention the fact that there were presents from almost all of Aiden's family scattered around the room. Maya might be gifted, and sounded older than her years, but she was still eight years old and adored the Disney princesses.

The room had been painted an antique white, and it was adorned with every Disney-princess item of décor that probably existed, from the rug on the floor to the bedside lamps.

Aiden had presented her with a princess necklace right before we'd brought her upstairs for bed. I was fairly certain it was white gold and not an inexpensive silver-plated one. And I was convinced that the heart with the crown above it was encrusted with real diamonds.

He'd told her it was a gift for his very own princess, which had made me want to cry.

He wasn't the least bit shy about letting Maya know that he cared, and that willingness to hold himself wide open to her had touched me.

Not that I ever allowed myself to weep. I hadn't for a long time. But his willingness to be vulnerable to his daughter almost immediately had drawn my emotions way too close to the surface.

"Are we going to stay here for a long time?" my daughter asked Aiden hesitantly.

"Forever, Princess," he answered emphatically. "You'll be lucky if I let you get married someday."

Maya let go of a delighted giggle that made my heart ache.

At that moment, I couldn't really regret the fact that I'd moved into Aiden's home, even though I hadn't really wanted to be a resident here. Maya was obviously happy, and she deserved the security of being in a gorgeous house that made her feel secure. But I was pretty sure it wasn't the nice home that meant everything to her. It was the fact that she had a father who adored her.

"Do you want me to read you a book?" Maya asked her father.

His laughter boomed in the large bedroom. "I thought I was supposed to read *you* a book."

I smiled. My daughter had been reading me a book every night since she was five. Because she was such an advanced reader, she preferred it that way, and she and I had always stopped to discuss the stories as we went along.

"I like to read," she answered simply.

"What are you reading?"

"I'm on the second Harry Potter book." Maya jumped up before Aiden could stop her, skipped to her bookshelf, and took the large softcover back to the bed with both hands.

Aiden turned his head toward me, and I shrugged as I said, "She wanted to start them three years ago, but I made her wait until they were age appropriate."

"She's already done with the first book?" he asked. "I've read them. They're long and probably not easy reading for a kid."

I hadn't forgotten how much Aiden loved to read anything and everything he could get his hands on.

I smirked. "She's read all of them several times already. She's working on another read-through of the series because she's gotten bored with The Lord of the Rings and The Chronicles of Narnia. She's read those two series so many times that they're all dog-eared. She loves fantasy. I did tell you that she was a gifted reader. But she doesn't get to read things that aren't age appropriate."

His eyebrows rose. "So she reads to you?"

I nodded. "She does. And we take breaks to talk about the stories."

He turned back to Maya, who had already scrambled back under the covers. "Okay, then," he agreed. "I'm lazy, so you can read to me."

My daughter laughed. "This isn't the way we do it. You and Mom need to come lie down with me and get under the covers."

Aiden looked confused, so I moved to the other side and slipped into the queen-sized bed. It was so much bigger than her usual twin, and there would be plenty of room.

I snuggled next to her and pulled the covers up, and then I gave Aiden an encouraging look.

He shot me a relieved smile and followed my lead on his side of the bed.

When Maya was sandwiched between the two of us, she finally gave both of us a satisfied nod and began to read.

Aiden interrupted occasionally, and acted out some of the scenes with fictional voices, making my daughter chortle like a child, a sound I had rarely heard.

"You're funny, Dad," Maya told him with a giggle after he'd finished a dramatic voice of the villain. "You do good voices."

I lifted my head as I saw the look of awe on his face.

Aiden had made it clear that Maya could call him Aiden. He obviously hadn't wanted to pressure her into accepting him as her father until she was ready. And I could tell that he was incredibly happy that she'd acknowledged him as her dad for the first time.

"I used to read to my younger brother and sisters," he told his daughter in a voice that was raw with emotion.

"Were you kind of like their dad, too?" Maya asked with curiosity.

"A little. I wasn't old enough to be their father, but I was their older brother. I was there to protect them and take care of them," he explained.

"I'd like to have a brother or a sister," Maya stated. "Now that you and Mom are together, can I have one?"

Aiden shot me a panicked look, and I smiled. It wasn't like I hadn't warned him that Maya was going to ask questions. A lot of them.

Aiden had explained to her earlier that he hadn't known that she existed until yesterday, and that if he had known, she would have always been in his life.

I'd been grateful that he hadn't blamed me. Instead, he'd chalked it all up to a misunderstanding between the two of us just like he'd said he would, and, blessedly, Maya had accepted his explanation.

But that didn't mean she was done asking questions.

I knew my daughter way too well to believe she was going to quietly be okay with the fact that we were all living in the same home.

"You'll have to ask your mom," he said in a husky voice.

I glared at him. "We aren't ready to talk about that, Maya," I answered. "We just want to enjoy time alone with you."

She nodded her agreement. "I want that, too. For right now."

Her words were a warning that she'd pursue the topic later. I knew how my child operated.

She was happy that we were apparently a family, and that bothered me, because we really . . . weren't.

Yeah, Aiden and I were both here, but we were far from being a loving family unit.

Would it be enough that Aiden and I just loved *her?*

Maya returned to her reading, but my mind wandered.

It hadn't been a bad day. In fact, it had been just the opposite. We'd spent the afternoon out by the pool, and then we'd barbecued outside for dinner.

It had been one of the most relaxing days I could remember.

But I could still feel the distance between me and Aiden, and it wouldn't be long before Maya would be able to feel that, too. She was sensitive and easily tuned in to other people's emotions.

Right now, she was over the moon about having a real father. But after the initial novelty wore off, she'd be bugging us to do everything together like a normal family.

I sighed. We'd have to cross that bridge when we came to it. But I had no idea what the solution would be.

Maya was the only thing Aiden and I had in common.

Maybe we can eventually learn to like each other. But I just can't marry him. I never want to be married again.

My first marriage had been hell on earth, so I wasn't about to step into the wedded state again.

It won't be long before Maya starts pushing to see Aiden and me get married.

In my daughter's mind, marriage would mean that she could have that coveted brother or sister.

Eventually, we'd have to tell her that a sibling was never going to happen. But I wanted her to get comfortable with having a dad and a new home first.

There had been way too much insecurity and sadness in my daughter's life. Today, Aiden had brought out the eight-year-old in her, and I was grateful for that.

He's good with kids.

Not that I had ever thought that he wouldn't

be. I'd seen Aiden with Jade when we were younger. He'd always been protective and supportive, and he'd given his siblings all the love he had to give.

Maybe that was part of the reason why I'd fallen for him so hard when I was eighteen.

He'd made me feel safe and important, too.

I startled as Maya closed her book none too gently. "That's the end of the chapter," she said with a yawn. "Can we read more tomorrow? I'm kind of tired."

"Get some rest, Princess," Aiden advised as he sat up. "Tomorrow is a school day."

"I wish I could just be with you," she told him hesitantly.

Aiden grinned at his daughter. "I'm not going anywhere. I'll be here when you get home."

The relief on my daughter's face made me want to cry. Maya really was afraid that Aiden would suddenly disappear from her life as quickly as he'd entered it.

Don't cry. I can never cry.

"I thought we could go to Disneyland next weekend," he suggested.

Her face lit up. "That would be so cool. Mom took me when I was younger, but I'd love to go now that I'm old enough to appreciate it and do some bigger rides."

My heart sank. Even though we were in fairly close proximity to the Disney park, I hadn't been able to afford to take Maya there for the last several years.

"Then we'll go," Aiden said with a grin, looking just like a little boy himself.

Maya tilted her head. "When did you last go?"

"I've only been there once, a long time ago," he confessed. "And it rained all day."

"Bummer," Maya commiserated. "This time will be better."

I sat up and rose from the bed. Aiden took up a seated position beside his daughter. "It will be fantastic," he promised.

There was silence before Maya asked hesitantly, "Can I hug you good night?"

My heart squeezed as Aiden opened his arms for her immediately. My daughter threw herself against his strong body and wrapped her arms around his neck trustingly.

The two of them stayed like that for so long that I thought Maya might fall asleep on her father's shoulder. But Aiden eventually lowered her back onto her pillow and kissed the top of her head. "Sleep, Princess," he said hoarsely. "I'll see you at breakfast."

He backed off so I could hug and kiss my daughter good night.

"I love you, Mom," Maya said as she enthusiastically hugged me. "Thank you for giving me a dad."

If I hadn't already known how much Maya

missed having a father, I realized it as I held her warm body against mine. "I love you, too, Sugar Bug," I said as I let her go and kissed her cheek.

I didn't trust myself to say anything more without bursting into tears.

Maya made herself comfortable, and I pulled the covers tightly around her.

By the time I went to turn off her bedside lamp, I was pretty sure she was already out cold.

She'd had a long day.

When I glanced at her for the last time before I plunged the room into darkness, I realized that my daughter had fallen asleep with a smile on her cherubic face.

It was pretty pathetic that I couldn't even remember the last time that had happened.

CHAPTER 8
Skye

"This was her baby picture," I told Aiden as I pointed to one of the first photos in the album I was holding. "It was taken right after she was born."

When Maya had gone to sleep, Aiden asked if he could look at pictures of the parts of her childhood he'd missed. He grabbed a beer, and I got a glass of wine before we sat down on the living-room couch together to look at her childhood photos.

"She's so damn tiny," Aiden remarked.

"She was big enough," I informed him. "Eight pounds, eleven ounces, and she was breech. I had to have a C-section."

"Was it painful? Who was there with you? Your ex-husband?"

"I had some pain after it was over, but I was so in love with our daughter that I didn't notice all that much. And nobody was there. It was just me and Maya."

"Nobody came to the hospital?" He sounded angry.

I slowly shook my head. "No. I told you that nobody really acknowledged Maya."

"How in the fuck can anybody be that cold?"

I wasn't about to tell him just how cold the Marino family could be. Not having them at Maya's birth had been nothing to me. In fact, I'd been relieved.

"It didn't really matter," I said hastily. "I had my daughter. And things were awkward with my in-laws. They hated the fact that Marco had married a woman who was pregnant with someone else's child. I think I was more relaxed being alone. I was nervous, anyway. I had no idea how to take care of a baby."

"The nurses helped?"

"A lot," I acknowledged. "They taught me all of the routine stuff, and once I got home with Maya, I got over worrying about hurting her if I did even the slightest thing wrong. But I was still a young first-time mother. I guess some fears never go away. I still get concerned over every cold or case of sniffles she gets."

"I'm sorry you went through all that alone," he said hoarsely.

"I lived through it," I replied. "Oh, this is her first birthday." I pointed to a picture on the next page.

"God, she looks so much like Brooke when she was little," he said as he reached out and touched the edge of the picture.

"She looks like you," I said softly.

"I guess she does," he said in an awed tone.

"I'm sorry you missed all those years."

"I'll make it up to her. To be honest, I'm sure I probably would have lost it when she was a baby. I would have been even more freaked out than you were. I don't really remember my younger siblings being babies. Mom was still around back then."

I flipped the page once Aiden had glanced at all the visible photos. "They're so small that it's pretty intimidating. But it seems like she's growing up way too fast now."

I kept explaining all the pictures he was seeing, and we sat like that for a long time, just looking at Maya's childhood images.

Finally, I got to the end of the book. "I have some others that I haven't had time to put into an album yet."

Aiden took the pictures and put them on the coffee table as he said, "All this was hard on you, Skye. I can understand that now. You were way too young to be alone, much less alone with a baby."

"I wouldn't trade what happened for the world," I assured him. "I love Maya, and I can't imagine not having her in my life."

He looked frustrated as he answered, "If I had only gotten that letter. I would have been there."

I put a hand lightly on his forearm. "I know."

And honestly, I *did* know that now. Seeing my daughter with her father made me recognize just how serious Aiden was about family, and how readily he'd always taken on whatever responsibility he felt he needed to shoulder.

If he'd known, he would have been there. I'd just been too disappointed and hurt to realize it when I'd been eighteen.

I glanced at the clock. "I have to go. I need to go close up at the café."

He looked at me, his expression confused. "Now? It's late."

"I always close. All of my staff is part time. Most of them are college students. I don't have anybody who knows how to close things down."

"You can't be there alone," he said stubbornly. "It's late, and it's not safe."

I stood up. "Aiden, this is Citrus Beach. And it's not tourist season. It's pretty quiet after dark."

He rose. "It's a big-enough city to have our share of crime."

He was right. Citrus Beach was growing, and bad things did happen here occasionally. Honestly, I didn't love being in the café at night after all the employees had departed. There was money to count, and accounting to do. So it made me uneasy. But I'd kind of gotten used to it.

"I'll be fine," I told him.

"You'll be great, because I'm coming with you," he stated stubbornly. "And tomorrow we'll look at hiring you a manager. You said you wanted the restaurant to be more. So make it *more,* but don't plan on ever being alone there again at night. It's not safe."

I wanted to say something. I really did. But the fact that he was actually concerned about me kind of overrode my indignation about him telling me what I could and couldn't do.

Nobody had ever cared whether I was safe or not.

And the warmth that flooded my body because someone cared felt so damn good.

"You don't need to go," I argued weakly.

He swiped his keys from the end table. "I'm going," he said in a voice that said he wasn't compromising. "And you better start thinking about what you want the café to be. Maybe we could just close it down while it's getting remodeled rather than hire right now."

"Aiden, I can't do that. That's my livelihood."

"You don't need it," he said firmly. "I'm a damn billionaire, Skye. I can take care of you and Maya."

"Taking care of me wasn't part of the deal," I retorted. "And I want you to get to know Maya. I'm not here so you can take over the expenses."

"I'm making it part of the deal." Aiden moved so he was blocking my way to the front door. "You need to take a break. I'm not saying that you need to stop being Maya's mother. But you need to take care of yourself. I can see how damn tired you are, and I hate the fact that all of the responsibility of raising Maya has fallen on you without help from anybody."

"I've never complained about that," I argued.

"I'm complaining for you, then," he rumbled. "You need a goddamn break, and I'm here now. Maybe I wasn't before, and I regret that. But now that I'm around to watch over both of you, I'm not going to let you work yourself to death."

I knew I should be telling him I'd do whatever I wanted. But if he pushed the issue, he'd win anyway. "We'll need to compromise."

"I'm open to that, as long as you stop working almost every hour of every day. You need to put yourself in a creative position instead of being responsible for all the day-to-day stuff."

I sighed. "I'd love to see the Weston Café become the in place to eat instead of a greasy-spoon diner. But it needs to be more on trend. Healthier, fresher food. Vegetarian options. And a décor that makes people feel good and want to come back again."

"You can change everything, Skye. Completely remodel and reinvent the entire restaurant," he urged.

I wanted that so much. "I'd have to do a significant investment."

"You got it," he replied immediately.

"Aiden, you don't need to do that."

"I want to," he insisted.

I tilted my head to search his face. He wasn't

lying. He really did want to help me, for some reason I couldn't put a finger on. "We need a written agreement. You can become a partner."

He moved forward until I could feel the warmth of his breath on my face. "You and I are going to be permanent partners. We're getting married."

I swore that my heart nearly stopped as I saw his tenacious expression. "We haven't agreed on that yet," I answered breathlessly.

"We will," he vowed. "I'll be good to both of you, Skye."

For a moment, he reminded me of the old Aiden, my big, buff, obstinate fisherman that I'd loved so damn much. The only person in the world who had ever wanted to protect me from all of the bad things that could happen to me.

He's not that man anymore.

I kept trying to convince myself that the Aiden I knew was gone. But really, he hadn't changed all that much.

He was still resolute when he wanted something.

"The only thing we have in common anymore is Maya," I asserted.

"That isn't the only thing we still have," he said as he wrapped his steely arms around my waist.

"W-what are you talking about?" I stammered.

I was mesmerized by the fire I saw in his beautiful eyes.

"You feel it, too, Skye. So don't bullshit me.

We have this." He lowered his head and covered my mouth with his.

I hadn't experienced desire in over nine years, so it stunned me that I responded almost immediately.

Wantonly.

Desperately.

Longingly.

I wound my arms around his neck as he plundered, exploring and seizing my lips like they belonged only to him.

I lost my practiced composure almost immediately as my previously dormant body roared to life just from the feel of Aiden's soft lips and demanding embrace.

When we finally came up for air, I put my head on his chest, and I could hear his heart beating in the same rapid rhythm as my own.

"We still have that," he rasped next to my ear.

"Sex isn't everything," I answered weakly as I pulled away from him.

He let me go. "Maybe not, but it's definitely *something*."

The doorbell rang as I was still trying to catch my breath, and I stayed put while Aiden moved out of the living room and headed toward the foyer.

He was back within moments, but he wasn't alone.

"Skye, meet Hastings. He's my caretaker for

the property. He's going to hang out here until we get back, in case Maya wakes up."

I shook hands with a silver-haired man who gave me a genuine smile as he remarked, "It's been a while since my kids were young, but I think I can handle the little one if she needs anything."

I realized that Aiden must have texted his estate manager to hang out at the house to babysit.

"Thank you," I said sincerely as I took my hand back.

I wasn't worried. I knew Aiden wouldn't leave Maya's well-being to anybody he didn't completely trust.

I was so used to my neighbor dropping over to watch out for Maya while I closed the café that I hadn't even thought about the fact that if Aiden was going along, I'd need someone to be at the house with my daughter.

Plus, I was pretty certain that his kiss had temporarily scrambled my brain.

"Happy to help," Hastings answered with a warm smile that put me even more at ease.

We were out of the house in moments, but I didn't want to admit that it felt nice to have somebody come with me so that closing the café wasn't quite so lonely.

CHAPTER 9
Aiden

I was a truck kind of guy. Always had been. When you grow up fishing, it helps to haul equipment with a truck.

As we drove toward downtown, I had to wonder, now that I was a family man, if my big-ass truck was really the best vehicle for a guy with a kid.

Sure, I'd bought a nice, shiny, brand-new truck with a king cab when I'd come into a lot of money, but I wasn't at all sure about the safety statistics on carrying an eight-year-old in it.

But I knew I was going to look it up when I got back home from taking Skye to close up the café.

Jesus! How in the hell had Skye ever gotten through those first eight years? I'd been a father for all of one day, and I was a wreck about what was and wasn't safe for Maya.

"Who's named as her father on her birth certificate?" I asked as I got on the freeway.

"You are," she said into the darkness of the truck's interior. "If anything ever happened to me, I wanted to make sure that she'd go to you. I guess, even back then, I knew you'd take care of her if she had no other family."

I balked a little—or maybe a lot—at the thought of anything happening to Skye.

Nothing will ever happen to her or Maya. I'm here to make sure it doesn't.

I was having a harder and harder time being pissed off at her. After having spent some time with my daughter, I knew that Skye was a fantastic mother. She'd brought Maya up right, and the love she had for our daughter was right there for anybody to see.

Yeah, I fucking wished she'd come back or called, after leaving that letter, and made damn sure that I knew I had a child. But she'd been little more than a kid. Barely eighteen. And considering her background and lack of help, she must have been terrified to find herself pregnant with no real way to provide for either herself or our baby.

She could have hit me up for child support the moment she found out I'd inherited a massive fortune.

She'd known I was rich, but had never asked for a damn thing.

And God knew she could have used some help after she'd gotten back to Citrus Beach. She'd taken care of Maya the only way she knew how . . . by working herself half to death.

"Why didn't you ever hit me up for child support?"

Her soft sigh drifted through the cab of the

truck. "Why would I ask you to support Maya when I thought you didn't give a damn whether she existed or not?"

"Most women would," I pointed out.

"I'm not most women. Maya and I have survived alone since she was born. We managed."

"I know it was all a misunderstanding," I said. "But I feel guilty as shit because I wasn't there."

"Don't," she said immediately. "I didn't know I was marrying into an infamous crime family back when I wanted you to come for me. But looking back, it probably wouldn't have been safe for you if you had come. Marco was ruthless about getting what he wanted. And he wanted me."

I wanted to tell her that I wouldn't have given a shit who I had to face down to get to her and our child, but I let the comment slide. "Did he treat you good? You said he ignored Maya, but what about you?"

"He wasn't a nice man," she said carefully. "He was having some kind of midlife crisis, I think. He thought a trophy wife would help, I guess. My duty to him was to make sure I always looked perfect and stayed by his side whenever we went somewhere. But he never wanted me to make conversation. He didn't see me as a person at all. I was pretty much just a possession."

"What an asshole," I cursed.

I couldn't imagine a guy having a wife like

Skye and not treating her like she mattered.

"Luckily, he kind of lost interest in showing me off after a year or two," she answered without any discernable emotion. "And I was glad. I got to spend more time with Maya instead of twisting myself in knots trying to make him happy."

"When did you know what he really was?" I asked.

She was silent for a few moments before she answered. "I think I always knew something wasn't right. He was out more at night than he was during the day, and it seemed strange that he could conduct a legitimate business that way. The first thing I realized was that his so-called church wasn't exactly a safe haven. His family *used* the church to find victims for human trafficking. They promised runaways the world, and then enslaved them. Some of them were just teenagers. Once I realized that, I was able to look at *everything* he was doing and figure out that there was drug running, money laundering, and a myriad of other illegal activities happening, too. I never saw any of the murders, but they happened. If somebody got ready to rat them out or betray anyone in the family, they conveniently disappeared."

"Fuck, Skye! Why in the hell didn't you leave?" It made me half-crazy thinking about Skye and Maya being in that atmosphere.

"Because leaving would have been more

dangerous than staying," she informed me. "People don't leave the mob. Those are the ones that just . . . disappear."

She was probably right. She'd had nowhere to go with Maya. Which made me feel even shittier than I already did.

"Did he ever touch you?" I questioned.

"In what way?"

"Any way," I grumbled. I didn't want to hear about her sex life with another guy, exactly, but I was curious what her life had been like.

"Having sex with him was horrible," she said honestly. "He was brutal, and all I wanted every single time was for it to be over. He didn't give a damn if he hurt me. And yes, he got irritated with me and slapped me around plenty of times. But I gladly took it because I'd rather he vented his anger on me than on my daughter."

"Son of a bitch," I rasped, furious that anyone would touch her in anger.

If the bastard wasn't already in prison, I'd be tempted to go after him and teach him a lesson about how a man treats a woman.

"It's over, Aiden. I lived through it," she said gently.

"No wonder you don't want to get married again," I said.

"That's why," she replied. "Nobody is ever going to own me again. No one is ever going to tell me how to live."

Well, hell, I kind of did want to own her, but not in the way that Marco had.

Mine!

I'd always had a visceral, primal reaction to Skye, but it was because I wanted her to be safe and protected. I didn't want to tell her what to do. All I'd ever wanted was for her to be happy after the shitty childhood she'd had.

"Not every man is going to be like that," I told her.

"I know. But you're already trying to get me to give up my restaurant."

"I don't want you to *give it up,*" I denied. "I want you to take some time to relax. I want to see you less exhausted. And I thought you wanted to spend more time with Maya."

"I do," she said in a harsh whisper. "And I have to admit that I'm tired. But you can't just order me to do things, Aiden."

"I'm kind of used to giving orders," I admitted. "I was a senior crew member when I was out on fishing jobs. And when I came home, I was parenting my siblings."

"I'm not a kid anymore," she reminded me.

Didn't I fucking know that! Skye had gone from a pretty young woman to a mature gorgeous female who had my dick perpetually hard.

"I'll try to ask more often rather than telling you what to do," I agreed reluctantly, knowing that when it came to Skye and my daughter, it wouldn't be easy not to insist they do whatever was the safest and easiest way to accomplish things.

Maybe it was a little weird that my protective instincts toward Skye were still so prevalent. But they weren't going away, so I'd have to learn to roll with it. She was the mother of my child. So it might be totally normal to feel that way.

She had a smile in her voice when she answered. "That would be nice."

"Don't ever be afraid of me," I insisted. "I'd never hurt you or Maya. I might be an asshole at times because I want you both to be safe and happy. But I swear I'd never touch you in anger."

I wasn't the type of guy to *ever* hit a woman in anger, and I wanted to make that clear. That kind of behavior was for fucked-up cowards.

"I know," she said simply.

I was silent as I pulled into the parking lot of the café. After I'd thrown the truck in park, I asked, "Do you want to tell the crew that you're shutting the restaurant down for a while? I still think you should make it what you want it to be."

"I want to make it different than it is right now," she considered. "I'm afraid that if I don't change it, the café will become obsolete. Citrus Beach has been changing for a while. It's a small beach city that's been growing like crazy. Trendy eateries are popping up everywhere. The place needs some specialties. It needs to be rebranded."

110

"But?" I could hear the hesitation in her tone.

"It's a lot to ask for you to become my partner and invest in a place that really needs a lot of work. But if I don't do it, I might have to close it down eventually."

I tightened my hands on the steering wheel. "If you'd take it, I'd happily gift you the money, Skye. But if being your partner is the only thing you'll accept, then I'll do it."

I already knew she was way too proud and ambitious to take something for nothing. Hell, she could have collected a boatload of child support, something she was entitled to get, and she hadn't even done that.

So I'd compromise. This time. I didn't much care what it took to get her to eat more and work less.

No woman should look as weary as she did most of the time.

"Thank you for believing in me," she said softly.

"I know you can do it," I said sincerely. "I agree completely with your assessment. And I don't want you or Citrus Beach to lose the café. But it needs a whole new brand to stay relevant."

Even though it was annoying that I couldn't get her to let go and trust me, I totally understood why she wanted her independence. She'd never had any kind of security in her life.

I wanted to give her the café that would keep

her feeling independent. I never wanted her to feel trapped again.

"Then I accept," she said firmly. "I'll let the crew know."

I smiled even though she couldn't see me in the dark cab.

That was one victory won, but it hadn't come easy.

However, she trusted me a little, and for right now, that had to be enough.

CHAPTER 10
Aiden

I jerked on my tie the next morning as I made my way downtown. I hated feeling like I was being strangled by a tight noose around my neck, and I was itching from the heavily starched shirt I was wearing.

I wasn't a custom-suit type of guy like Seth and Eli Stone.

But we met with potential partners and clients in our offices, so we had to look like professionals.

To be honest, I wasn't really ready to see Seth's face right now. But it was Monday morning, and I'd promised I'd be at the office.

Business was booming, and I had an obligation to the company.

I need to let Seth know I've made some decisions.

Sometimes, I really wished I enjoyed the thrill of the acquisitions and the projects that were under development.

At first, the whole idea of working in partnership with Seth had been appealing. But I'd pretty much discovered that real estate did nothing for me.

I'd rather be fishing.

I'd rather be in a pair of jeans and a comfortable shirt.

I'd rather be making a bigger difference in the world now that I had more money than I could spend in a lifetime.

It wasn't like I didn't appreciate the fact that my siblings and I were now filthy rich. But the transition had been . . . difficult.

When a poor guy suddenly realizes that he could never work another day in his life but he'd still keep getting richer from his investments, it's daunting.

I liked to work.

I was used to busting my ass for small pay and long hours.

But the only thing I was good at was fishing.

So Seth's idea to work together had sounded good at the time.

Too bad that I just didn't feel like I fit into the whole real-estate environment.

I needed to be outdoors to feel normal, and the ocean was in my blood.

Once I'd parked my truck at the Sinclair Building, I got out and pulled on my suit jacket.

Strangely, I actually smiled as I locked up my vehicle, because I still remembered Skye telling me how handsome I'd looked this morning before I'd left the house.

Hell, I knew I reacted to her praise like an

infatuated high-school kid, but I couldn't seem to stop myself.

We'd both taken Maya to the bus stop, and I'd enjoyed a great breakfast because Skye had done the cooking.

I didn't miss my usual solitude in the morning, that was for sure. I *liked* having them both around.

I entered the lobby and raised a hand to the security guy at the front desk as I pushed the button on the elevator for the top floor.

At the moment, Sinclair Properties was only occupying the entire upper floor. But I knew that Seth had ambitions that would fill the whole building with company employees very shortly.

Once I hit the offices, I passed by mine and made my way to Seth's next door.

He was standing behind his desk, and I didn't hesitate as I walked up to him. Once he turned his head and looked at me, I hauled my arm back and slugged him in the face so hard that he landed flat on his ass.

"What the fuck, Aiden?" he whined from his seated position on the carpet. "I think you broke my damn nose."

I flopped down in a chair in front of his desk. "She was pregnant, you asshole," I informed him angrily. "She left a letter to tell me that she was having my baby."

I watched as Seth got into his chair and reached

for some tissues. The blood hadn't landed on his pristine suit yet, but it would if he didn't stop the bleeding from his swollen nose.

"How in the fuck would I know that?" he questioned grumpily. "That thought never even occurred to me back then. You were always careful. You weren't the kind of guy to get a female knocked up."

"It didn't matter. You should have never screwed with my mail. It changed a lot of lives, and not for the better. Skye was miserable, and my daughter was not in a great environment."

I hated to admit it, but I kind of enjoyed watching his nose bleed and swell up. The bastard deserved it.

Seth held the tissues in place, only removing them once the bleeding had been stanched.

"So I'm the enemy now?" he asked while he stared at me unhappily.

"You're my brother," I corrected. "I just don't like you much at the moment."

"I didn't know, Aiden. I swear. I would have told you if I'd read it."

"My life would be entirely different if you had let me know," I drawled. "And so would Maya's and Skye's. Maybe they would have had less material things, but I believe that neither one of them cared about that. They just wanted to be safe and loved."

"Maya and Skye?" he asked. "Skye's daughter is *your* child?"

I nodded and then proceeded to tell him the whole story.

When I'd caught him up, I added, "By the way, I quit. I'm done with Sinclair Properties. This is *your* dream, not *mine*."

Seth shook his head. "You don't mean that. This company is already worth eight figures, and it won't take long before it's even more."

I shot him a warning look. "Believe it. I plan on turning over full ownership to you."

He gave me a look of disgust. "You're just pissed right now—"

"That's not why I'm doing it," I interrupted.

"Then why in the hell would you give up a company that's kicking ass right now?"

I shrugged. "It's not my thing. I don't get a hard-on from dealing in properties or land. And high-rises do very little for me."

"Jesus, Aiden. You can't just—"

"I can," I assured him.

I started to think about what Skye had said about people always telling her what to do, and I could relate.

"Somehow, I can't see you lying on the beach with a beer for very long," Seth warned.

"Neither can I, which is why I'll be working on my own company. I'll start in my home office and see where it goes."

"What's your plan?" Seth asked.

"I want to amass one of the biggest

seafood-supply companies in the world. I want to build a fishing empire. What I can't get myself, off the boats I plan to launch here, I'll source from fishermen around the world. I have a ton of contacts. And I want it all to be done with *sustainable* fishing. I'll use the guys who do it the right way. No more bycatches."

Even though I'd always loved fishing, there was too much waste and too many species that were caught and killed without being our targeted catch. If my grandkids were going to be able to still get protein from the oceans, there needed to be more responsible fishing.

"You seem to have it all figured out," Seth said flatly.

I nodded. "I've been thinking about it for a while."

I could provide a ton of jobs in Citrus Beach, and I could also do fishing the way it should be.

Not that I planned on going out again for long-ass trips. I could find great captains and crews to man the boats.

Building up the name would take a lot of work, but I was up for the challenge. In fact, I knew I'd relish it.

"If that's what makes you happy, I think you should do it," Seth said grudgingly. "But maybe we could swap your part of this business for half of your fishing empire. I'd like a piece of it. I could run Sinclair Properties, and you could build your business. But we'd be partners in both businesses."

"I'd have to think about it," I said in a noncommittal tone.

"You're still pissed?" he said, astonished.

"Not really," I shared. "Busting your face and watching you bleed helped."

"That's cold," he shot back.

"You don't exactly give me a warm, fuzzy feeling right now," I rumbled. "What you did was stupid. And it caused Skye a lot of pain she didn't deserve."

"Agreed," he said in a hoarse voice. "If I could go back and change it, I would. But I can't change the past."

"I can't either," I conceded. "All I can do is work for a better future. Skye and I are going to get married."

Okay. Yeah. I knew she hadn't agreed *yet*. But she would.

He gave me a cautious look. "You want to get back with a woman who left you for another guy?"

"I told you. She had *nowhere else* to go," I said, knowing it was the truth now. "And I never saw that damn letter."

She'd thought I'd abandoned her.

So she'd had no choice.

"If it makes you happy, then I'm glad," Seth said as he threw the tissues away.

His face was swollen, but the bleeding had stopped.

I nodded. "Thanks."

"So when's the wedding?"

"As soon as I can convince her to marry me."

"She said no?" Seth questioned.

"The only thing she agreed to was moving into my house so I could get to know Maya."

"You're stubborn enough to convince her," he said drily.

I stood up. "I hope so."

"Where are you going?" Seth asked as he rose from his chair.

"Home," I decided.

"I was hoping you might hang out and help me."

Since I was used to never saying no when my family needed me, I asked, "What do you want help with?"

"We got a prime piece of real estate down by the water, but we can't build. Some tree-hugging lawyer is having a fit because it's the nesting place of some endangered bird species. The California least tern or something like that. She called early this morning. I have a feeling she's going to be a pain in my ass."

"Conservation is important. I think Jade would agree." Our sister was a die-hard wildlife conservationist.

"Don't tell Jade," Seth requested with something that sounded an awful lot like panic. "She'd be all over my ass."

"Maybe you could just make the land a sanctuary."

Seth glared at me. "I bought the real estate to develop. It's right on the water. I'm not willing to lose that kind of money."

"I'd kick in. Those birds are at pathetic numbers."

"Not. Happening," he answered obstinately.

"Then good luck developing," I told him as I strode toward the exit.

"Aiden," he called.

I stopped as I reached the door to look back at Seth.

"You can't stay mad at me forever."

"I'm sure I'll get over it."

Time would be my friend. Eventually, the hell of listening to every bad thing that had happened to Skye would stop. Or at least I hoped it would get easier.

"I'll miss you being here," Seth confided.

"It was never really my thing," I said, letting him off the hook. "But it's always been your dream. Don't give it up."

"No way in hell," he agreed.

"Give the tree hugger a break," I suggested. "It isn't going to hurt you that much to give up the property."

"For a bunch of birds?" he said roughly. "Hell,

no. We can just arrange to get them moved."

I grinned because I couldn't help it. "I think Eli will agree that it should end up a sanctuary, since he's marrying Jade."

"We'll see," Seth said ominously. "I don't think he became one of the richest guys in the world by having a bleeding heart."

Really, it didn't matter how my soon-to-be brother-in-law had gotten rich before. Eli Stone was crazy about Jade, and he'd back her in a heartbeat. If my little sister got wind of the fact that there were rare birds that needed to be saved, Seth would never hear the end of it.

"Good luck getting Eli to back you up," I said, still smirking as I walked out the door.

I was pretty sure that Eli Stone would rather go broke than make my little sister unhappy.

It was the primary reason I liked the guy so much.

CHAPTER 11
Skye

I was surprised to see Aiden come through the door of his house a little more than an hour after he'd left. "You're back early."

I was seated at the breakfast bar with a cup of coffee, looking over ideas for the café. I watched as Aiden moved to the coffeepot and made himself a cup, too.

It wasn't difficult for me to see that his right hand was swollen, since I loved to watch those capable hands do almost any task.

I stood up and walked over to him. "What in the world happened to your hand?"

I took his hand in mine as I examined it.

"No big deal," he grumbled. "It just connected with Seth's face. Well worth the pain."

I was suddenly alarmed, and I looked up into his ocean-blue eyes, searching for the truth. "Is that really what happened?"

I turned his hand over and over. It was pretty swollen, but he seemed to have a full range of movement. I finally gave his hand back to him after I was satisfied that most likely nothing was broken.

"He deserved it," Aiden said hoarsely. "If he

hadn't decided to burn that letter, things would have been way different. Maybe I wouldn't have had a lot of money, but you and Maya would have been cared for by people who gave a damn."

"In all the years I've known Jade, I've never seen a single Sinclair lay a hand on another one," I mused.

"Usually we don't," he said as he ran his injured hand through his hair, leaving it spiking in a couple of places. "This was a special circumstance."

I felt sad that I'd caused a rift between him and Seth. "I'm sorry this happened. I know how close you are. And I think he was only trying to be helpful, even though he was misguided."

"I'll get over it someday," he said. "But right now, I can't forgive and forget. This shit is too raw. I hate what happened to you, Skye."

I sighed. I couldn't blame him for being confused and angry. He'd missed way too much of his daughter's life. But it really touched me that he'd obviously been ticked off about what had happened to my life, too.

"It's over, Aiden. We can't go back and redo it. Maya is a healthy, normal child. Both of us made it out of our situation relatively unscathed."

Yeah, there were a few issues. The fact that I couldn't seem to show my emotions out in the open came to mind.

And Maya hadn't been raised in the best

environment, even though I'd tried my hardest to shield her from the truth.

But I was determined to move on from my past.

He shot me a turbulent look. "Did you really come out unscathed?" he asked huskily. "You protected Maya. But who in the hell protected you? He beat you up, Skye. And he beat you down. You barely show any emotion about any of that."

"Because I never could," I said truthfully. "Showing emotion was a weakness I couldn't afford, Aiden. Please understand that it isn't that I don't hate the bastard I married and divorced, and that I'm not pretty damn happy his ass is going to sit in a federal prison for the rest of his life. But being in that life meant that I could never let him or his family know how I felt. It wasn't possible without consequences. He'd take those feelings and use them against me. I'm so used to being numb that I don't know how I feel about anything except Maya."

I was breathless by the time I'd finished. I hadn't meant to blurt out my confusion to Aiden, but it seemed important that he understood exactly where I was at emotionally.

I didn't know how to feel *anything,* and the sooner he understood that, the better we'd get along.

I didn't know how to be happy. I'd been in survival mode. I hadn't felt any kind of *joy* since that summer I'd been with him.

I didn't know how to be truly sad.

I didn't know how to really connect with other people, because I'd been so isolated.

It wasn't like I didn't crave connection, but for me, trusting anybody was dangerous.

Aiden must have sensed that I was conflicted, because he did the most extraordinary thing. He opened his arms wide.

Instinctively, I threw myself into them without a thought.

And nearly broke when he wrapped those strong arms around me protectively.

I basked in the warmth and protection of his muscular body as I rested my head on his shoulder.

Aiden was an enormous man. I might be tall for a female, but the top of my head barely reached his mouth.

But for some reason, we always fit together perfectly.

"I care what happened to you, Skye," he rasped against my hair. "I care that you had nobody to be with you when you were eighteen and pregnant with my child. I'd like to kill Marino myself for ever laying a hand on you. I can't help the way I feel."

I closed my eyes and tried to absorb Aiden's strength. The man had more conviction in his little finger than many men had in their entire souls.

We stood in the kitchen, wrapped around each other for so long I lost track of time.

I felt stronger when I finally backed away, like being close to him had given me some of his strength.

"I'm really sorry about Seth."

He shook his head as he picked up his mug of coffee. "Don't be. It made me do a lot of thinking about where I'm headed in the future. How do you feel about being married to a fisherman?"

My eyes shot to his. "What? You *are* a fisherman, Aiden. You always will be. It's something you love."

Not only had Aiden caught fish for a living, but it had always been a passion for him, even when he wasn't working. I was never fooled into believing he went recreational fishing just to help feed his family. He'd always loved the sport.

"I'm leaving Sinclair Properties to Seth, and I'll be starting up my own seafood-supplier business," he said as he looked at me, apparently to see what my reaction would be.

"Oh, my God. That's fantastic. Tell me about it," I said excitedly.

Aiden laid out his plans and answered all my questions.

He concluded, "It will help the city provide more jobs, and the whole model is based on sustainable fishing. No more killing species inadvertently. We have to use only what we need.

If I open a processing plant outside the city, and we do our own fishing from here for the species we can get here, it would provide a hell of a lot of jobs for Citrus Beach."

I laughed. "You've convinced me. If I had any money, I'd invest. What do you do about getting the seafood you can't get here?"

"I hire some damn good people around the world to source stuff for me that's caught sustainably."

I was quiet for a moment before I said, "You look happy."

He nodded. "I am. As handsome as you think I look in a suit, I'm not really that kind of guy."

I hit him playfully on the arm. "You look handsome in anything. You know that. And the whole blue-collar billionaire thing is pretty appealing."

He shot me a sideways glance. "You think so?"

I nodded emphatically. "It's especially nice that you'd be doing something you care about."

I hadn't bothered to argue about the fact that we hadn't agreed on the marriage part of our deal. At the moment, it didn't matter. Aiden had been through a huge life change, and he needed to get comfortable with his switch of business.

"Seth and I haven't worked out the details yet, but I may take him up on his offer to stay as a silent partner in Sinclair Properties in exchange for him having a silent partnership in Sinclair Seafood."

"That's the official name of the new business?"
He nodded.

"I like it," I agreed.

"I'll start out working from my home office. I have a lot of building to arrange, and boats to purchase. The marina was just expanded, so it should work to house the boats for now."

"Since I won't have the restaurant open for a while, I'd like to help however I can. I don't have that many skills, but I'd do anything you needed," I offered.

I wanted to do whatever I could to get Aiden's business off the ground. He looked so happy, and I wanted him to keep smiling.

He gave me a playful grin. "Just the fact that you think I can do it helps. And I wouldn't turn down some assistance. I'm not exactly organized."

"Perfect," I said as I smiled back. "I'm kind of anal about laying out plans. So I'll help you get things together. I honestly think starting two new businesses will be fun."

"It will likely be hell," he warned.

"It won't. It will be a challenge."

There was something about Aiden and me doing this together that brought me a sense of excitement I hadn't experienced in a long time.

"I'll help you, too," he promised. "But can we start work after Maya goes to school, and wrap it up at dinnertime? I was serious about you taking a break."

My heart skittered. Aiden had actually asked me like I was a partner instead of bossing me around. Not that I thought the concession would last forever, but he'd heard me when I'd said I'd rather be asked than told.

"I'll break a little before that to get dinner together," I offered. "Deal?"

He folded his beefy arms. "Did you really think I was going to argue about not cooking?"

I laughed. "I like to cook." I suddenly remembered something. "Speaking of cooking, I have to make cookies for Maya's class this afternoon. It's her turn to bring treats. Chocolate chip is her favorite."

"I used to just buy stuff for my younger siblings," he considered.

"Times are changing," I explained. "I do healthier cookies with oat flour, coconut sugar, and less chocolate chips."

"I think I'd prefer the old-fashioned ones," he grumbled.

I snorted. "Me too. But the healthier ones aren't bad. And I still make the real thing for Maya sometimes. I just try to be careful with the real sugar, and make sure to mix the healthy stuff with the treats."

"She's a good kid, Skye. You did a great job with her," he said as he looked at me.

My heart warmed as I saw the genuine look in his gorgeous eyes. Nobody had ever really told me that I was doing things right with Maya. I'd always been terrified I'd do something to ruin my child, since I'd had absolutely no child-raising experience.

"Thanks," I shot back at him with a smile.

"Can I help with the cookies?"

"Do you really want to?" I asked, my heart beating just a little bit faster.

I kept telling myself not to make too much of having a partner to help raise Maya. But it felt good just the same.

"I really do," he confirmed.

We finished our coffee and proceeded to make some healthier chocolate-chip cookies together.

I had a hard time keeping most of the chocolate chips out of Aiden's mouth, and there was oat flour everywhere by the time we were done.

But I hadn't laughed so much in years, and I was still chuckling once the entire kitchen was clean again.

CHAPTER 12
Skye

The week leading up to Jade and Eli's wedding was one of the most amazing periods of time I'd ever experienced.

Aiden took to being a father almost naturally.

I couldn't say that he exactly spoiled his daughter rotten. Thankfully, he never made me the bad guy when I had to enforce bedtimes and rules. In fact, he backed me up completely, and even reminded Maya when there was something I'd asked her to do.

But he *was* a sucker about giving her anything and everything she wanted, for the most part.

Luckily, my daughter wasn't the type to ask for anything extravagant.

"My piano teacher says I'm learning so fast that I could probably do a recital this summer," my daughter said excitedly from the passenger seat in the new vehicle Aiden had mysteriously bought. I had a hunch he'd felt the sudden need for an Audi A3 more for my benefit than his. But since my old jalopy was prone to breakdowns, I'd happily taken the loaner he'd offered.

I shot my daughter a quick sideways smile.

Since she was almost nine, I let her sit in the front now.

"She thinks you'll be able to play a whole song?" I asked.

"That's what she said. I hope I can. I'd love to play for you and Dad."

My heart squeezed painfully. If it wasn't for Aiden, my daughter wouldn't be doing piano lessons. She'd only recently started, but she'd always wanted to learn. I just hadn't been able to afford to send her to private piano study. It was extra money I'd simply never had.

But the moment she'd mentioned her wish to Aiden, it had been granted. He'd asked me first, but I had no reason to deny my daughter what she wanted.

As promised, we'd spent last Saturday at Disneyland, and the adults had experienced just as much fun as Maya had. The weather had been perfect, and Aiden had arranged the VIP experience, so we'd gotten onto every ride we'd wanted.

Maya had been so exhausted that she'd slept the whole way back home.

"You'll do great, Sugar Bug," I told her. "You always accomplish whatever you want to do."

"I love playing piano, Mom. And I really like having so much family. Even Uncle Noah offered to take me to SeaWorld this summer. And Uncle Seth said we could go to the zoo."

Because she has her uncles and aunts wrapped around her finger. Even Seth.

I had no doubt that Maya was eating up the family attention. She seemed to adore all of her new relatives.

"Be careful that you don't ask for too much, Maya. Your aunts and uncles have very busy lives."

She was thoughtfully quiet for a few moments before she asked, "How much is too much? They offered and I said yes."

I nodded. "Then it's okay. That means they want to take you. But don't ask them for things, okay?"

"I wouldn't," she said. "You always told me not to ask for things from other people. Maybe my real family is different, but it wouldn't be polite."

Sadly, I had always requested that she not ask her stepfamily for anything. And she'd understood the situation way too well to ever talk to any of them.

Sometimes, Maya seemed so much older than her years. "You're such a good girl," I complimented her.

"That's what Dad told me, too," she said with a sigh. "But it's not really all that hard. I think it's easier to be good than bad."

I bit back a laugh. I was pretty sure all parents wished their children thought that way.

I pulled into the winding driveway of Aiden's

home with a sigh. If I had to pick a dream home, his mansion would be it.

It was imposing with its beautiful brick exterior and large windows, but not so grandiose that it was unwelcoming.

And he had an enormous pool, plenty of land, and a hot tub.

I hit the garage-door opener and pulled into one of about seven stalls. My old vehicle took up one, and Aiden's truck another. The third was now occupied by his new black Audi, but the rest were unoccupied.

Knowing Aiden, he'd probably been too busy to fill the garage with boy toys or fancy cars.

I picked up some groceries from the back seat before I followed Maya into the kitchen entrance.

"Dad, what are you doing? It looks like a bomb went off," Maya observed with a giggle.

My eyes widened as I looked around the room.

Something smelled good, but the kitchen looked like a massacre had taken place.

There was red stuff all over the countertops and the large stove.

I bit my tongue as I saw the sheepish, harried look on Aiden's gorgeous face.

"Spaghetti night," he told us. "I always did spaghetti night when my sisters were young. I guess I kind of lost my touch."

"I'll help you, Dad. Mom and I do spaghetti sometimes," Maya offered as she went to the sink and rinsed out a dishrag to wipe off the counters.

"Damn jar exploded on me," he said as he looked at me with eyes that were pleading for guidance.

"Happens to the best of us," I said in a soothing voice. "It smells good."

I took the big spoon out of his hand and watched the noodles, while Aiden and his daughter wiped up the kitchen.

Really, in all the years I'd been cooking, I'd never had a jar explode its contents all over the kitchen, but poor Aiden looked so frustrated that I wasn't about to tell him that.

I was way too flabbergasted that he'd even tried to make dinner. I was also more than a little emotionally moved that *he cared* about screwing up dinner.

I tasted the sauce. "It needs . . . something."

Maya grabbed the Italian spices and brought them to me without me even asking. We'd been a team for so long that she knew what I wanted.

"Does it taste like shit?" Aiden asked as he tossed his dishrag in the sink.

"Not at all. But I think it needs more oregano. It's good, Aiden. No worries."

I was tempted to remind him that if dinner got screwed up, we could always order out. But he seemed too freaked out about not being able to feed us. And the sauce was good. It just needed a few more spices.

I added a few things, stirred it, and pronounced, "All done. Thank you, Aiden."

I dished up a plate for Maya, and she carried it carefully to the table and then went to get silverware for everybody and a glass of milk.

"She does all that stuff herself?" he asked in a voice that wouldn't carry to his daughter.

I turned my head and smiled. "Of course. She'll be nine before too long. She's pretty helpful, actually."

"I noticed," he said with a grimace.

"You don't have to impress her, Aiden. And you don't have to be perfect. We all screw up sometimes, especially me. Kids don't come with instructions. But no matter what you do, she's going to adore you anyway." I kept my voice low so my daughter didn't hear our adult conversation.

"I want her to know she can count on me," he rasped.

"She already knows that."

"I can't even make her dinner without screwing it up."

"She loves McDonald's," I informed him. "Happy Meals work."

He lifted a brow. "Are you trying to make me feel better?"

I shook my head. "I'm just giving you my secrets to raising a daughter. Be flexible. It helps."

137

"You're right," he said, sounding relieved. "I didn't need to lose my shit over spaghetti."

"It wasn't the dinner," I told him. "You're doubting your skills as a parent. And it won't be the last time. I still have my moments. But she's turning out just fine."

He shook his head as he grinned. "I guess we're lucky she's so easy to please."

I dished up a plate and gave it to him. "Go eat. I'm looking forward to the spaghetti myself. I'm starving."

I quickly put away the few things I'd picked up at the store and joined Aiden and Maya at the table.

My daughter was telling her dad about her day at school and her piano lessons.

And her father was watching her like he was riveted to every single thing she did that day.

Didn't he know that he was giving Maya everything she wanted or needed?

He was giving her attention.

He was showing her that he loved her.

I knew my daughter, and she needed those two things a whole lot more than she needed a perfect dinner.

Aiden was being a father, and Maya's delight was evident.

"I have a pretty pink-and-white dress to wear to Aunt Jade's wedding," Maya informed her father. "I'm probably a little too old to be a flower girl, but she's letting me throw rose petals anyway."

"I didn't know you were in the wedding," Aiden answered as he demolished the food on his plate.

"Jade asked her when she asked me to be her bridesmaid," I told him. "I got her a premade dress, a hat, and some gloves that Jade and I picked out. She would have hated sitting still long enough for a custom dress."

"You'll look like a princess," Aiden said with a wink at Maya.

"I'm not wearing a crown, Dad," she said.

"Then you'll look like *my princess,*" he corrected.

"Do you want to see my dress?" she asked hopefully.

"I can't wait," he answered patiently. "But finish your dinner first, and let your mom eat. We'll see it afterward."

Maya beamed at her father, and my heart tripped.

My daughter had finally found her father, and he was her hero.

Problem was, I was pretty sure I found him to be just as much of a conquering warrior as she did.

CHAPTER 13
Skye

I had to bite back a moan as I slipped into the outdoor hot tub completely naked.

Aiden had gotten on a call with Seth after we tucked Maya into bed, and I'd grabbed a towel and made my way outside.

I'd made my escape to the tub a couple of times now, when Aiden had been occupied later in the evenings.

But my threadbare one-piece swimsuit had given way to a huge rip down the front a few days ago, and I'd had to toss it.

I should have made time to get another one. But I hadn't gotten to a department store or Walmart to get something yet.

Still, the warm jets of the hot tub had been beckoning me.

So I'd just grabbed a towel, certain I could get in and out of my jeans and T-shirt fast enough if I had to.

There were several entrances into the pool area, but I'd crept out through the dining room, and I'd left the outdoor lights off. So all I had for light was that coming from inside the house.

Not that I cared.

I liked the quiet and peace of the outdoors after a busy day.

I sank into the warm water up to my chin, allowing the jets to soothe away the tension in my back and neck before I took the lounge seat.

I closed my eyes and absorbed the relaxation, but it didn't last for long.

I jumped just a little as I heard a door sliding open, and my eyes flew to the same door I'd exited.

I quickly realized Aiden didn't even know I was in the dark hot tub, watching every move he made, even though he was only a few feet away from me.

He set down the beer he was holding on a small table next to a lounger, and proceeded to strip himself down.

I couldn't have said a word aloud if I'd wanted to. I was speechless.

The long khaki shorts dropped to the cement, and he pulled the polo shirt he'd been wearing over his head and added it to the pile.

My breath caught as he shucked his boxer briefs and stood in the light from the house.

Aiden was a gorgeous specimen of manhood. But naked, he was simply . . . beautiful.

Muscles rippled beneath tan skin, and as I gawked at his stomach, I could see the defined six-pack abs that had always made me drool. His cock was half erect, and I ogled it as my mouth watered to take a forbidden taste of the man I was yearning to have.

I bit my lip as I eyed the strength of his shoulders, back, and tight ass that I wanted to grope more than I wanted to breathe at the moment.

The air left my lungs with a giant *whoosh* as he dived into the deep end of the pool.

If I wasn't already warm enough, an incendiary heat infused my entire body and landed painfully between my thighs.

I wanted Aiden.

I'd always wanted him.

But now I was mature enough to recognize the furious desire.

I was silent as I watched him do lap after lap, his arms cutting through the water so easily that his actions appeared to be effortless.

I need to tell him I'm here. I'm spying on him.

Oh, who in the hell was I kidding? I was doing more than that. I was staring at him, imagining what it would be like to have that gigantic cock buried deep inside me again after so many years.

It would be . . . sublime.

But it couldn't happen.

He confused me.

He confounded me.

And he made me feel way too much.

After he finished his laps, he pulled himself out of the pool gracefully.

"Aiden," I whispered longingly, wishing I could touch him just once.

"Skye?" he said as he turned toward the hot tub. "Is that you?"

Caught!

I had no idea whether he'd managed to actually hear my nearly silent uttering of his name, or if he just sensed my presence.

"I'm sorry," I said in a raw tone. "I didn't want to disturb you."

God, that's a lame excuse.

"I wanted—" I shut my mouth before I got myself in trouble.

I was surprised as Aiden breached the distance between himself and the hot tub without a single bit of shyness. "You got an eyeful by staying quiet," he said huskily. "What did you say you wanted?"

I let out a squeak as he flipped on the light and lowered himself into the hot tub. "I'm naked," I said in a panic.

"Me too, sweetheart," he said with naughty humor in his tone. "But I think you already noticed that."

The water was now heavily illuminated, and it was a little bit disorienting at first.

The last thing I wanted was for anybody to see me naked. I had some stretch marks, and the incisional scar across my belly from my C-section wasn't pretty.

Still, I couldn't take my eyes off Aiden. He drew me toward him without even touching me.

He frowned. "You look upset."

"I'm not. I just don't get naked with people," I snapped at him.

"If we get married, we're going to see each other naked," he said patiently.

Even though we'd had a child together, Aiden and I hadn't really seen each other nude. Our encounters were usually fast, and in a place where completely taking our clothes off wasn't an option.

"W-we aren't getting married," I stammered. "I told you I don't want to get married."

Aiden moved quickly across the small space between us. "Skye? You looked scared. Take a breath. It's just me. I'm not going to hurt you."

My fear was crushing me. I knew I was over-reacting, but I couldn't help the anxiety that was rising to the surface.

"Come here," he said gently as he wrapped his arms around me. "You're shaking, baby."

Aiden didn't know that any sexual act that had happened to me over the last nine years had been rape. Yeah, some people might say a husband couldn't rape a wife, but none of them had ever been brutalized by a man who was more animal than human.

The arms holding me now were warmly familiar.

144

This is Aiden. He'd never hurt me.

Without letting me go, he took the lounge seat in the hot tub and rested my body on top of his. I straddled him, which made me feel safer, and I began to calm as he stroked a big hand over and over up and down my back.

"What was all that about?" he said huskily beside my ear.

"Bad memories," I said in a tremulous voice.

"You know I'd cut off my arm before I hurt you, right?" he asked.

I nodded against his shoulder. "I know that. But sometimes I get flashbacks. I was treated for PTSD after I filed for divorce. It's never quite gone away."

"Shit, Skye!" he rasped. "I didn't know. What can I do to help?"

"Have sex with me," I pleaded. "Make me have memories that are good again."

I hadn't meant to request that he fuck me, but it seemed like the only way I'd ever get some of the horrible images out of my head.

"Fuck knows I want that more than I want almost anything," he said gutturally. "But not like this. Never like this. Not when you're afraid of me."

"I'm not afraid of *you*."

"Look at me, Skye," he demanded.

I pulled back and met his eyes. They were dark, deep blue, and filled with heat.

"See *me*. Not *him*."

I nodded slowly, the tension leaving my body. "I do."

"Kiss me," he requested. "Please."

My heart skittered as I leaned closer, and I felt the heat of his breath on my lips.

He was asking, giving me control. And I wanted to sink into Aiden more than I wanted to be afraid.

I opened my mouth and let my lips touch his. Instinct took it from there.

He didn't make any quick movements. He just kissed me back, our lips and mouths sliding against each other's sensually.

Finally, I speared my hands into his wet hair and just held on as he took control.

His breathing was heavy as his mouth slid down the wet skin of my neck. "Jesus, Skye! I want to touch you, but I don't want to do the wrong thing."

My senses were full of Aiden now, and there was no room for anything or anyone else. "Touch me," I said with a tiny moan. "Please."

He reached between our bodies greedily, and I backed up to give him space.

I gasped when he cupped my breasts and teased the nipples with his thumbs. "Yes," I hissed as I sat back on his legs, and he sat up.

My entire body ached with tension, but I wasn't scared.

There wasn't a single moment that I could doubt who was making my body come alive. Only Aiden had ever been able to work me up like this.

I arched my back as Aiden took a nipple between his lips and nipped. As his tongue stroked over the hard peak, white heat raged over my body.

I nearly exploded right then.

"I ache, Aiden. So bad," I said as I shivered.

"I know how to make it go away," he said persuasively.

"Do it."

His hand slid down my body, and I drew in a sharp breath as his fingers stroked over my pussy.

"Yes. Yes, please," I whined.

I needed Aiden to touch me, to make the pain of longing go away.

He probed and found my clit, and every touch made the pressure rise.

"Ride me, Skye," he said roughly. "Take what you need."

I'd never had a man satisfy me except him, and our couplings had been frantic. We'd never taken the time to really touch each other much, those few times we'd actually had sex.

Now he was offering me everything.

And I took it.

I pressed my hips hard against the big hand that was pleasuring me, grinding against him, ecstasy flowing over me from getting the sensation I really needed.

I began to ride him harder, and our eyes caught and held as I felt my orgasm building.

I couldn't tear my gaze away from the ferocious look in his eyes.

He wanted me to come.

His stare demanded that I come.

And I became frenzied as I felt his need match mine. I ground against him harder, desperate to orgasm.

My climax hit me, and waves of pleasure washed over me so hard that I could barely breathe.

I fisted his hair and kissed him, my tongue twining with his as my orgasm finally subsided to a few ripples.

When I released his lips, he said in a raspy voice, "That's how it should feel, baby."

I sighed and collapsed against his shoulder, knowing this was one memory I could live over and over again without a tiny bit of fear.

"Thank you," I said breathlessly.

"My pleasure," he grunted as he scooped up my body and took us both out of the hot tub.

He dried me off, and he carried me to my bed completely naked.

Only when I was alone, after he put me into my bed, did I remember that he hadn't really had *his* pleasure at all.

CHAPTER 14
Skye

Jade and Eli's wedding day turned out beautifully. Luckily, the weather had cooperated, since the whole thing was taking place on the beach in front of their adjacent homes.

Elegant white tents had been erected the night before, and the sand had been smoothed down to allow for the aisle and altar.

My daughter had tossed her rose petals with abandon, and every woman had cried over the amazingly romantic ceremony . . . except me, of course, since I never let anybody see me cry.

But just because I hadn't given in to tears didn't mean my heart wasn't light as I watched my best friend hitch herself to the man of her dreams.

Jade was happy, and I was happy *for her*.

The only part that made me sad was the fact that, once Jade and Eli returned from their extended honeymoon in Australia, my best friend would be primarily living in San Diego. Jade was opening a research lab there, and all of Eli's offices were in the city.

It wasn't that San Diego was actually far away. I could make it by car on a good traffic day in about an hour. It just seemed like a distance because Jade wouldn't be around that often to hang out with me in Citrus Beach.

"Having fun?" Aiden asked as he put a hand lightly on my shoulder from behind.

I turned to smile at him. God, he looked gorgeous in a tuxedo. And I was beginning to like the way that he always seemed to want to touch me whenever he saw me.

"It's a lovely reception," I said. "Where's our daughter?"

I was waiting at the bar in the food tent to get a drink.

"The princess is currently talking her uncle Seth's ear off," he informed me with a grin.

Aiden flagged down a waiter, ordered us both something, and then turned around again to stare at me.

"Something wrong?" I asked.

"You look beautiful, Skye. Did I tell you that today?" he asked in a husky tone.

I wasn't exactly shy, but I was pretty sure I blushed. "Twice," I reminded him.

He shrugged. "You look so nice that it's worth saying again."

My heart squeezed. I'd lived with a man who acted like he mostly hated me for years, so it lightened my soul to see the sincerity in Aiden's eyes.

"Thanks. You're looking pretty handsome your-self. Maybe you're not crazy about wearing a tie, but the tux looks good on you," I said.

He grinned. "I don't mind since I know I don't have to wear it every day."

"So what were you doing?"

I hadn't seen Aiden since the ceremony had ended an hour ago.

"I was helping set up some of the musical equipment."

"Xander is doing a few songs, right?" I asked.

Jade's cousin Xander Sinclair had once been a superstar of rock and roll. Now, he was doing more production and mentoring of new artists than performing himself. And his record label and the rising stars he was showcasing had taken off like crazy.

"After I do my little thing," he confirmed.

I looked at him. "What *little thing?*"

He shrugged. "Jade wanted me to sing and play her wedding song, 'All of Me.' She used to love it when I sang to her when she was a kid."

I was stunned. "I had no idea you could sing. What do you play? Guitar?"

"Piano. We had a rec center when I was younger. They had an old piano there, and some people who offered free lessons. Seth plays guitar. He still has the beat-up one he's owned since we were kids."

"But you don't own a piano now," I observed, still shocked to learn that Aiden had musical talent.

"I'm rectifying that since Maya loves to play. It's being delivered on Monday."

"You're buying her a piano?"

"I'm buying myself a piano," he corrected. "But of course, she's free to use it whenever she wants."

I shot him a skeptical look. "That's just a tricky way of saying that you're buying her one, and you know it."

After the waiter gave us our drinks, Aiden asked, "Is the trick working?"

I let out an exaggerated sigh. "How can I tell you what you can or can't put in your house? Do you really play?"

"You'll see for yourself shortly. I'm not going to rival John Legend, but I can hold my own."

"I love that song," I shared right before I took a sip of my cocktail.

"Then I'll sing it for you," he answered in a low, sexy baritone.

My heart skipped a beat. "It's Jade's wedding song," I protested.

"She's going to get her song of choice."

"I can't wait to hear you sing. I can't believe I never knew you loved music so much."

He shrugged and tossed down half his drink, which looked like some kind of whiskey. "I always meant to buy a piano. Seriously. I just hadn't gotten around to it. The rec center closed a few years ago, so I had to find a friend with a piano so

I could practice the song. It's been a while since I've actually played. And I don't generally do it in front of a crowd. But when your little sister asks you to sing a song for her special day, you do it."

"I've actually never seen Xander perform in person, either," I mused.

"He sucks," Aiden said drily. "I never understood why he packed houses around the world."

I rolled my eyes. "You don't mean that."

"Of course I don't," he confessed. "He's a music genius."

I slapped his arm playfully. "Jealous?"

"Naw. I just like to give him hell when his head gets too big."

I laughed. "I guess you like most of your newfound family?"

"Most of the time." He swallowed the rest of his drink and set the empty glass on a nearby table. "I guess I better get moving."

I slurped down the last of my own drink and set the glass next to his as he took my hand. I followed him as he tugged me through the crowd and outside.

I immediately noticed that the stage that had been set up last night was totally lit.

The dance floor might be sand, but the stage looked like it was hosting somebody pretty important.

"Wait for me?" Aiden asked. "I want to dance with you as soon as I'm done."

I stopped near the stage. People were already crowded around it. "I'll be here," I told him breathlessly.

I watched as Jade and Eli stepped up to the mic.

The two of them did the usual thanking of everyone for sharing their special day.

My mind wandered as I looked around the stage for Maya, and then found her sitting on her uncle Noah's shoulders.

It was the first time I'd seen the ever-serious Noah smile.

Seth was standing next to his older brother, talking to Maya, and I could see that she was having a good time with both of her uncles.

I was glad that Seth and Aiden were back on speaking terms and were working out exactly how the ownership of the businesses would go. I'd felt bad that I'd driven any kind of wedge between them.

But I knew that Aiden was happier since he'd started planning out how he was going to execute the plans for Sinclair Seafood.

I put my attention back on the stage as I heard the beautiful chords of the piano start, and I noticed Eli and Jade leaving the microphone to take the dance floor.

I was captured by the piano intro, but I was completely mesmerized when Aiden started to sing the emotional song, every note pronounced and stunningly poignant.

Aiden put himself into performing the music, portraying everything that the song was meant to say.

He kept tabs on me by looking at me frequently, and it nearly made me break down into tears.

That's how good he was.

He glanced at me and winked, and my heart almost flew out of my chest because it was beating so fast.

Thump-thump!

Thump-thump!

Thump-thump!

I could hear the rapid rhythm pounding in my ears like it was measured to the beat of the song Aiden was belting out.

It was surprising when the tune started to crescendo, and another male voice sang along in harmony near the end of the song.

Xander.

He wasn't in the spotlight, but was sitting on a stool in the dark on the other side of the stage.

Shivers ran down my spine as I absorbed the words of the song and the emotion that was threaded through the notes.

And then there was silence, and a burst of enthusiastic applause that I joined once I got over my shock.

It was clear where my daughter had gotten her musical talent.

And it sure as hell hadn't come from me.

CHAPTER 15
Aiden

I hopped down from the stage, not caring if it was going to kill me to dance with Skye.

I'm doing it anyway.

I wanted her.

I needed to have her soft, silken body plastered against mine.

Since my dick was constantly hard when she was within sight, what the hell did it matter if I was actually touching her or not?

Maybe I was a masochist, but I knew I couldn't resist the chance to have her that close to me.

"Dance with me," I said, forgetting that I was supposed to be requesting things from her.

I wasn't giving her a chance to say no this time.

I needed to feel her in my arms. I needed to know she was safe. That no bastard was ever going to touch her again—except me. Maybe I was a dick sometimes, but I sure as hell would never hurt her intentionally. And just the thought that someone had tortured her for years nearly made me come unglued.

She reached for my hand, but I took her arms and wound them around my neck, and then pulled her whole body to me by locking my hands behind her waist.

Luckily, Xander had started one of his moody ballads that made our position work perfectly so we swayed to the music, our bodies perfectly in tune.

"You were amazing," she said, sounding slightly breathless. "And you were wrong. You don't *rival* John Legend. You're just as good, with your own style."

I put my mouth against her hair. "Thanks for the vote of confidence, but I'm an amateur, and I've never wanted to play or sing for anybody but family. It's just a hobby."

"Are you saying you never had dreams of fame, even when you were younger?"

"That's exactly what I'm telling you, sweet-heart."

"Too macho for music?" she teased.

"Nope. I just don't like performing in front of a crowd. I give guys like Xander credit for their balls. They're willing to put themselves out there. But it's not fame that drives my interest. I just . . . like doing it."

"Nothing wrong with that," she answered with a sigh. "I like to do needlepoint, but I've never wanted to sell my work. So I get it."

"Some things we just do for fun."

"But . . . well . . . you're pretty good at your fun stuff," she said softly.

"I'll play for you and Maya anytime you want," I offered.

A light bulb appeared to go on in her head. "You could actually teach Maya."

I shook my head. "No. She needs to learn the right way. After I got the basics from a few volunteer teachers, I was self-taught. I do a lot of things by ear. She's better off with a real music teacher."

"Ah, well, she likes her new teacher, anyway," she answered. "It's good for her. I never really had the money to let her do many extra things. And when I was married to Marco, I was afraid to ask for anything."

Fuck! I hated the fact that Skye had ever been so damn scared that she couldn't ask for something for our daughter. And probably nothing for herself, either.

This beautiful woman had lived in a prison without physical bars, but a situation that was, in reality, a hell of a lot worse than being in a real detention center.

I closed my eyes and breathed in Skye's tempting, flowery scent, an aroma that was so uniquely hers, and so damn alluring that my cock was at full attention and begging me to get her naked.

And I hated my damn treacherous dick. It wasn't that all of me didn't want that, too. But not now. Not until she was comfortable.

It was obvious to me that Skye was used to any kind of touch being ugly, savage, and cruel.

I wanted to teach her pleasure again. But I couldn't do that until she completely trusted me.

And I wasn't about to let my cock do my thinking.

"I wish you had never stayed with that bastard," I said before I could monitor my words. "I mean, I get why you did. You were worried about Maya's safety, and your own. But fuck, Skye. You didn't deserve what happened to you."

My vision clouded with rage just thinking about some man touching her with anything except devotion, love, or passion.

Hell, if I wanted to be honest, I couldn't stand the thought of another guy touching her *at all*.

But the way Marino had treated her was callous and heartless.

"If there's one thing I've learned, it's that life isn't always fair," she said with a resigned sigh. "Was it fair that your mother died when you were all so young? Was it fair that you had to struggle financially to raise your siblings and essentially lose your own childhood? Was it fair that you couldn't chase your dreams as an adult?"

"That's different. None of us were physically hurt."

"Sometimes the other stuff is worse than the physical pain," she said wisely. "It lasts a hell of a lot longer."

She was right. I knew she was. "Why didn't

you tell me that you suffered from PTSD before? What are your triggers?"

After getting her off in the hot tub, watching the beauty of her face as she reached her climax, leaving her alone in her bed had been one of the hardest things I'd ever done. But I hadn't known what to do. I didn't want to screw up the progress we'd already made.

Over the last few days, I'd been studying PTSD, and I still didn't know what scared her.

Of course, she wasn't easy to read, since she buried her emotions.

She was different from the girl I knew so long ago, yet some things remained the same.

Like the way she tangled my dick up in knots.

"I'm better," she murmured against my shoulder. "I went through counseling, and I worked on the issues myself. I didn't want to have a million little triggers. It wasn't healthy, especially for Maya."

"This isn't about Maya. This is about you. What scares you, sweetheart?" *Jesus!* I really wanted to know.

"Not much triggers my reactions anymore. Really. I'm okay."

So she was going to blow it off?

"If I can't touch you without you having flashbacks, you're *not* okay."

"You're touching me now," she pointed out in a soft voice.

"You know what I mean." Hell, I didn't want to sound like a dick, but I wanted so much more information than she apparently wanted to give up.

"If something bothers me, I'll always tell you from now on."

"You better," I warned.

It was so damn hard to be pissed off at her. She'd been through hell, and the last thing she needed was for me to push her.

"Maybe we should just have sex," she whispered. "Maybe it would help."

Shock kept me silent. "What did you just say?"

"You heard me."

"You think that's the answer?" I said, my voice sounding raw.

No way was I ever going to say no to her offer. I couldn't. I wanted her too damn much. But I wasn't sure this was the way it should happen.

"Marry me and we'll have as much sex as you want. Any way you want," I offered.

I was grateful when Xander floated into another ballad so I could keep Skye exactly where she was. But I was holding my breath, just waiting for her answer.

I was done denying that I didn't want this marriage for myself. That I wanted it for Maya. I wanted the woman in my arms more than I'd ever wanted anything else in my life. Selfishly. Just because I needed her to be mine.

It wasn't for my daughter, although it would be nice if we could be a real family.

I wanted Skye.

Period.

"Sex first," she murmured. "What if I can't do it? And I already told you that I don't want to be married again."

"You weren't *married* the first time. Not a real marriage, anyway."

Skye hadn't had a marriage. She'd been a jailed detainee.

"I need to be whole again, Aiden. I don't know what I'll want after that, but I need to be completely free of my past."

The longing in her voice made me cave in. I couldn't force this woman to do something she couldn't do with her whole heart. It wouldn't be fair.

"Then I'll take the sex. For now," I grumbled.

"What if I can't—"

"You can," I interrupted. "You just need the good experiences to outweigh the bad."

"How do we do it?"

I smirked into her hair. "I don't think you need me to teach you *that*."

"Actually, I do. We were only together a couple of times, and everything after that was bad."

"It wasn't your fault."

Nine years ago, I hadn't really had the chance to romance Skye, and I regretted that. She'd deserved more. But I was determined to make up for every fast screw I'd ever given her when we were young.

She sighed. "I had your child. And I was married for years. And I still feel like I don't know much of anything."

My cock was so hard that it was physically painful. "You have a very willing teacher," I assured her. "But let's figure out your trigger stuff first, and not just with the intimacy issue."

"I've never quite figured out how to not be afraid all the time," she confessed. "I've just learned not to let it show."

Hell, she might as well have knifed me in the chest. That's how goddamn bad it hurt to hear that it was hard for her to ever really relax her guard.

"Why?"

"Because there wasn't a single minute of my marriage that I wasn't afraid that Marco would figure out what was happening and snuff me out."

From what she'd said, Skye had tried to be a model wife. Why would Marino want her dead? "What did you do except try to please him?"

She lifted her head and looked around. There wasn't another couple close to us, but I had a feeling she didn't want anyone to hear our conversation.

"I did plenty that would make him kill me in a heartbeat," she said breathlessly.

I couldn't imagine what a woman like Skye could do to any guy that would make him want her to disappear. Fuck knew I couldn't comprehend that. I never wanted her out of my sight.

"Like what?"

She was silent as she laid her head back down on my shoulder, her mouth as close to my ear as she could get it. "I wasn't just docile and obedient during my marriage," she admitted.

"So you fought him?"

"In the only way I could. Aiden, I figured out what was happening in the family right after Maya's first birthday. And once I knew, I couldn't stay silent."

Holy shit! "You confronted him?"

"Worse."

I shuddered at the thought of her risking her life by telling her ex-husband that she knew he was into organized crime. "What the hell could be worse than that?"

"Once I knew, I couldn't just let it happen. I went to the police. They sent me to the FBI because they were federal crimes. I was an informant for several years. I'm the reason that the Marino crime family all ended up in jail for life. And I spent every minute of the day terrified that they'd find out. Once the FBI promised me that if anything ever happened or if I was compromised they'd make sure Maya was safe,

I started telling them everything I knew or could find out."

The truth finally slammed me over the head with a sledgehammer.

Holy fuck!

She was right.

There was something worse and more dangerous than confronting the mob.

Skye Weston had been the FBI snitch who had brought the entire Marino organization down for good.

CHAPTER 16

Skye

I'd never told anyone that I'd helped bring down the Marino crime family. It wasn't something I was exactly proud of, but it had been something my conscience had demanded that I do.

It had also been the *only way* to make sure Maya and I were safe for the rest of our lives.

Women didn't leave a Marino male, and the ones who had before me had conveniently come up missing and were never seen again.

Given the choice between disappearing and being an informant, it had been a pretty easy decision. There was no way I was going to have my daughter reach adulthood having been raised in a crime family. She hadn't really understood much of what was going on when she was young—thank God! And I'd wanted to get her out before she could figure out that her mother had married the mob.

Aiden didn't say a word to me as he took my hand and led me down to the beach. It was deserted, and a safe distance from the reception.

"Are you serious?" he said as we stopped before reaching the water's edge.

There was a gorgeous full moon, which gave

me enough light to see his face. "Yes. I've never told anyone except you. I fed information to the FBI for five years before they finally had a big enough case to make sure every member of the family involved would go down."

He dropped my hand. "No wonder you have PTSD. I can only imagine how afraid you were."

"Every single day I was petrified that it would be the day that somebody found out."

"Did you have to testify?"

I nodded. "Of course. But I didn't care. Every trial got me closer to the freedom I wanted for me and Maya."

"What made you decide to do it?"

I took in a deep breath and let it out slowly. "There was a maid in our house almost all the time. She was there from the time I went to live with Marco until Maya was just a year old. I liked her. She was young, in her twenties, and she was one of the only people I could really talk to. Her name was Maria. One day she told me that she had seen an enormous stock of heroin and cocaine on the lower level, and that then it all disappeared. And she meant *a lot* of drugs. I think she was trying to warn me. Unfortunately, Marco overheard her talking, and he showed her out of the house. She never came back. I never saw her again. When I asked about Maria, all Marco said was that she'd never talk again. That's when I knew he'd killed her. I didn't ever mention her again."

"Jesus Christ!" Aiden exclaimed as he raked a hand through his hair. "Weren't you afraid he'd shut you up permanently, too?"

"I think he would have if I'd talked about it in the open. But I learned to keep my mouth shut around any of the family. I was terrified."

"So you just kept giving the information quietly to the police?" he asked.

"I went to the police first, and they brought in the FBI."

"How did you do it? How did you keep feeding them information not knowing when or if the family would find out you were the inside source?"

I shrugged. "I didn't have a choice. If they didn't *all* get put away, I'd have to be scared of whoever was left on the outside. I learned to hide my feelings incredibly well. I didn't cry, I didn't show emotion. So they never suspected."

"What about Maya?"

"She had no clue what I was doing. I kept her away from all that. I was pretty damn grateful when it was over. But it didn't really end until the trials were all done and I knew none of them would ever get out of prison during their lifetime."

He put his hands lightly on my shoulders. "You realize that what you did was insanely dangerous, right?"

"I knew," I admitted. "That's why I had to make sure that someone promised to protect Maya if anything happened. And that they knew where to contact *you*. I guess even back then I knew you'd never reject your daughter if I wasn't around to take care of her anymore."

His fingers tightened on my shoulders. "You were so damn brave, Skye. But it literally makes me sick to think about anything happening to you. There's so damn much that *could have* gone wrong."

I shot him a weak smile. "Then imagine how I felt. I spent a lot of time looking over my shoulder, which is probably why I have some lingering PTSD. That and the fact that I never knew what Marco was going to be like whenever he walked through the door."

"Why did it take so long to arrest them all?"

"They required some very concrete evidence. They didn't want to jump the gun and risk not having what they needed to put them all away. It was a long, frustrating process. But I just kept thinking about when Maya and I would finally be free. How much we could do together. How neither one of us would have to be scared again. Maybe Maya never knew the details, but she was always a little nervous. I think she could sense my fear over the whole situation."

Aiden wrapped his arms around me and held me tightly against him. I felt his big body shudder as he said, "Jesus! I don't know what to say to make anything better."

I wrapped my arms around his neck. "You don't have to. It's over, Aiden. Other than the fact that I still have some lingering reactions from trauma, I'm good. Maya and I are free of them now. Honestly, I'm not sure she'll ever really remember much of what happened. She was only six when they hauled the entire bunch of them off to jail. And I said as little as possible to her about it."

"She's doing fine," Aiden said huskily.

"I took her to a counselor, but she said Maya was well adjusted. Maybe she didn't get to do some of the things that I wished she could have, but I tried to keep life as normal as I could for her."

Aiden tightened his arms around me. "I'm not worried about her. You did a good job at shielding her. I'm more worried about you."

I sighed. It had been so long since anybody had cared about me that I wasn't quite sure how to handle his concern. "I'm okay. I really am."

"Then why did you just ask me to have sex with you?" he asked drily.

Okay. Yeah. Maybe it *hadn't* been the best of ideas, but I couldn't marry Aiden. However, I couldn't deny that I wanted him. I think we both needed to scratch that itch. Maybe then he'd realize that I wasn't exactly normal. That I didn't feel things like normal people did anymore. And I'd make a lousy wife.

"I guess it was pretty selfish," I confessed. "But I think it's something we both want. When you touched me in the hot tub, you made me feel things I haven't felt since I was eighteen. I want to love sex again. I want to feel good. The last thing I want is to remember what happened to me during those years I was married to Marco. I'd rather replace those memories with something better. I'd like to think about *you* instead of *him*."

Aiden stroked my hair absently. "I want that, too, sweetheart. But I don't just want to fuck you—although I want that pretty badly, too. I want you to marry me. I want us to be the family we always should have been."

"You know I'm messed up, Aiden. You don't want me to be your wife. Something broke inside me during those years. I'm damaged."

"You're not, baby. You just need some recovery time."

"I'll never be the same Skye you knew years ago," I told him. "I was young, stupid, and terribly naive. The life I led after I got pregnant and in the years after changed me. I can't be that new high-school graduate anymore."

Sometimes I wished I could go back to the days when I was a lot more innocent, but I couldn't. I'd seen too much, been through too much. My dreams had been shattered, and I'd learned to just survive.

I'd managed to endure.

But I hadn't been truly happy in a very long time. My only joy was my daughter.

"I can't be the guy I was back then, either," he informed me. "But you and I can be something better."

"When you touched me, I could feel again," I tried to explain. "I guess that's why I wanted . . . more."

"It's not like I don't want that, Skye. I fucking do. I think I've wanted you from the first time I really saw you as more than just Jade's friend, after you graduated from high school. I'm pretty sure that if you'd shown the slightest interest, I'd have been all over another relationship when you came back with Maya, even though I thought you'd dumped me the first time. I never forgot you, even though I sure as hell wanted to."

"I never forgot you, either," I said as I pulled back from him.

I reached into my dress and slowly pulled out the red tiger's-eye necklace he'd given me so long ago.

I pulled it over my head carefully and held it in my hand as I confessed, "I've worn this necklace constantly since you gave it to me. Maybe part of me wanted to remember us, even if it had turned out badly. I only took it off when I had to, like when I had my C-section."

He lifted his hand, and I dropped the jewelry into his palm.

"I always wondered if you kept it," he said distractedly, rolling the stone between his fingers.

"It was my most treasured possession—except for the daughter you gave me. I would have left it with the letter, had I known I wouldn't see you again before I had to marry Marco."

He grabbed the chain gingerly and lifted it back over my head. "I want you to keep it."

I let out a silent sigh of relief. I'd worn that necklace for so long that it was almost like it was part of me. "Thank you. But if you ever want it back—"

"I won't," he said tersely. "I gave it to the only girl I ever cared about enough to trust with it." He paused before he continued, "So, do we work out terms for this new relationship?"

"I think we should. You'll eventually want out—"

"For fuck's sake, Skye . . . *I'm* the one who wants to marry *you*. Do you really think I'm going to bail out?"

Once he figured out how broken and flawed I was, he was going to want more than I could ever give him. So yeah, he'd eventually want someone who was capable of more emotion than I could give him. "You might," I warned.

"I guess we'll just have to see," he conceded grudgingly.

My heart ached. All I really wanted was to give in and agree to marry him. I wanted Aiden. I always had. But I couldn't tether him to a woman who had no idea if she was capable of being happy in the future.

I'd only been truly free for a year. My counselor had told me that it would take a while to regain my trust in people and relationships. But I wasn't always so sure *that* was ever going to happen.

"What are your terms?" I asked.

"There's no other guy but me, for one. I don't share, Skye," he grumbled.

Like I'd ever think about any man *but him?* Not gonna happen. "Fine."

He folded his arms. "That's pretty much all I have. If you're mine, I'm pretty damn good. What about you?"

"I think I want to be the only woman for you, too. I don't think I could handle anything else."

"Done," he answered hoarsely.

"Is that it?" I asked nervously.

He snaked his arms around my waist and pulled me into his body again. "For now. I'm not going to tell you that I don't want more, but we can take this one day at a time if it helps you."

I nodded, my heart in my throat.

He tucked a stray lock of hair behind my ear. "I'll make you so damn happy that you'll never want to go anywhere else," he warned.

"I want to make you happy, too," I said in an uneven tone that was almost emotional.

"Baby, you make me happy just by being here with me."

I felt tears threatening, but I ruthlessly blinked them away.

Sometimes, Aiden said things that were so damn sweet that I wanted to drown in his words.

But I knew better.

I had to be strong. If this relationship didn't last, I'd be *forever* damaged. I could feel that in my soul.

He tilted my chin up, and I could *feel* the heat radiating off him.

The spontaneous combustion started the moment he laid his lips on mine.

"Aiden," I murmured against his lips right before he deepened the kiss.

That one word expressed all the longing that I'd been feeling since we'd met up again.

The passion.

The need.

The damn painful desperation that I couldn't quite hide whenever he touched me.

I fisted my hands in his hair, and gave back as much as I was getting.

If I couldn't communicate with words, I was determined to use my body to do my talking.

I closed my eyes as he thoroughly explored my lips, opening my mouth so he could ease the ache I had to be closer to him.

There was nothing I wanted more than to climb inside him and never come out. That was how badly I needed this man.

He was breathing heavy when he came up for air. "Christ, baby. You're killing me," he said with a groan.

His hands cupped my ass and pulled my hips against his so I could feel just how much he wanted me.

And I shivered as I felt his hard erection grind against my core. "Aiden," I whimpered as I tugged at his hair.

"Mom!"

I jumped away from Aiden as I heard my daughter calling my name.

"Saved from fucking on a beach by our daughter," Aiden said in a frustrated tone.

I ran my hands down my rumpled dress as Maya came toward us with her uncle Seth in tow.

"Later," Aiden growled as he backed away from me.

It sounded more like a promise than a suggestion, and I discovered that sometimes I didn't mind his bossiness at all.

CHAPTER 17
Skye

"I'm going to miss you so much, but I hope you have a fantastic time. I know how badly you've always wanted to go to Australia," I told Jade the next morning as we hugged.

Despite Aiden's warning the night before, there was no hot sex when we'd arrived home. I'd been so tired that I'd fallen asleep with Maya while she was reading to me. I found myself covered up the next morning and snuggled beside my daughter.

Soon after we'd gotten up, Jade had arrived to say her good-byes.

"I'll miss you, too," she said tearfully. "But I'll see you in a month."

I snorted. "I doubt you'll spend much time missing us back here in Citrus Beach when you're with the husband of your dreams."

We both sat down to drink our coffee at the table.

Aiden had gone with Eli to do some last-minute errands before the newlyweds took off.

"I've been so crazy busy with the wedding that we haven't had much time to talk," Jade said with regret in her voice.

I shot her a smile. "That's okay. I've been

helping Aiden set up his new business, and I've been looking at new designs for the restaurant, so it's been crazy here, too."

"How are you two doing?" Jade asked anxiously.

I hesitated before I answered. "We're good. I think we're both starting to leave the past behind so we can give Maya a good life."

"But there's more than just Maya, right? I mean, it's obvious that there's still something there between you and Aiden."

I was surprised. "Is it really obvious?"

She shrugged. "Maybe only to me. I'm crazy in love with Eli. So I recognize the subtle signs."

"We don't really know what's going to happen yet," I admitted.

"Maybe it's okay to take your time," she suggested.

"Really, we don't know each other anymore," I confessed. "We've both . . . changed."

"Of course you have. You were only eighteen when you got pregnant, Skye. And even though you haven't shared much about your marriage, you're not the same person you used to be. You're a lot warier."

I felt guilty. "It wasn't because I didn't want to tell you. It was just . . . painful."

Jade had always been the best friend I'd ever had, but I was ashamed of all the trouble I'd gotten myself into. I hadn't wanted to tell anybody the whole truth.

"I understand," she said gently. "I don't have to know every little detail to know that those experiences did something bad to you. But please don't be afraid of Aiden. He'd never intentionally hurt you."

"I know. But it's hard for me to trust anyone now."

"Give it some time. You and Aiden will end up together someday. It doesn't matter how long it takes to happen."

I raised an eyebrow. "Why do you think that?"

She winked. "Because I saw the way you looked at each other when he was singing. He got to you."

Jade was right. Aiden did *get to me*. And I wasn't sure if I should be terrified or relieved.

I wanted to feel things again.

I just didn't want to face those emotions as quickly as I had with Aiden.

"I think things are happening too fast," I shared. "For years, I trained myself not to feel anything to survive. I poured everything good into Maya, but that was it. I turned myself off to everybody and everything else. I had to, Jade. I did it to protect myself and my daughter."

"But you don't need to do that anymore, Skye. I get that you had to block out the bad things around you, but that's all over. You deserve to start living again, and not just for Maya. You need it for yourself."

I took a deep breath and then let it out. She was right. But Jade didn't realize just how hard it was to let go of defense mechanisms that had probably saved my life.

"I know," I answered. "But it's definitely going to take some time."

She smiled. "You have all the time in the world. I don't think Aiden is going to go anywhere."

"He's an amazing man. He always has been," I said wistfully.

Jade pulled a face. "Well, *he is* my annoying older brother, but I guess I have to agree with you. All of my brothers are pretty extraordinary."

"You adore him and you know it," I said emphatically.

"Yeah, I do. So try not to torture him too much," she requested, still smiling as she raised her mug to drink.

"I honestly don't want to torture him at all. But I can't let him bully me into things, either."

She set her mug down on the table. "He's pushing too hard? I know Aiden has a tendency to go after what he wants with a vengeance."

"God, I can't really say that he's *demanding* that I do things. Well, not very often, anyway. But he can be pretty persuasive."

Jade laughed. "I know. He got me to eat my vegetables all the time. And I sure as hell didn't want to. But he usually tried to bargain with Brooke and me."

"He hasn't changed much, then," I replied drily.

"But his heart is good."

"I know."

"So give him a chance," she requested. "Take it at your own pace."

"That's the plan," I confided. "Though sometimes I want to put the pedal to the metal with him, but then I get . . . scared."

"Relationships are pretty terrifying sometimes," she agreed. "My connection with Eli certainly never went smoothly. And sometimes I still can't believe he's my husband. *Me*. The little geeky animal lover. How did I end up with someone like Eli Stone?"

"He's lucky to have you," I defended.

Maybe Eli was one of the richest men in the world, but nobody was too good for my best friend.

She rolled her eyes. "That's what my family says, too. But it still seems surreal to be Jade Stone."

I snorted. "You'll get used to it."

"I suppose I will. But I never want to take Eli for granted. What we have is . . . special."

"You won't, Jade. You're not the type. You appreciate everything you have."

"So do you," she said confidently. "Just don't let your fears rule your life."

I nodded and then took a sip of my own coffee. Unlike Jade, I didn't have a husband who

181

would walk through hell for me. But that didn't mean that I couldn't appreciate the fact that Aiden wanted me, even though I was still kind of a train wreck.

"I think that I'm afraid he'll realize how much I've changed, and that will push him away," I mused.

"Maybe you aren't the same woman you were at eighteen, but none of us are, Skye. Experiences shape us all as we grow up. But you're still the same sweet friend you've always been. Nothing has changed that. Okay, you bury your emotions more, but you have good reasons to do that. Trust takes time. I think after what you've been through, I'd prefer you were wary than to trust every single person you meet."

"I just hope Aiden can be patient," I said uncertainly.

"Um . . . patience has never been his strong suit," she advised. "He's always pretty much known what he wanted, and then he tries like hell to make it happen."

I smiled because she'd just described her brother exactly. "He's stubborn."

"I'm not going to argue with that," Jade said with a smirk.

"Talking about me?" Eli asked from the door.

Jade shot out of her chair and ran to hug her new husband like he'd been gone for months.

And it was adorable.

Eli kissed her, and my best friend came away with her cheeks on fire.

Aiden came through the door with a grin. "You two at it again?"

"I can't help myself," Eli shot back at Aiden.

"It's time for you two to get moving on to the honeymoon. I don't really want to watch my little sister get groped."

"We're on our way," Eli said jovially. "Unless Jade needs more time with Skye."

"Nope," I spoke up. "We're good. But I'm going to want to see lots of pictures."

"You guys are about ready to go, too, right?" Eli asked.

"Go where?" I questioned, puzzled by his comment.

"You and Aiden are—"

Jade reached out and slapped her hand over her husband's mouth. "Time to go, Eli," she told him firmly.

I watched a silent communication between husband and wife that I didn't understand as Jade took her hand from Eli's mouth and he grabbed her hand. "So we're out of here," he said sheepishly. "Take care, both of you. We'll see you in a month."

Aiden frowned. "You better call. I want to know you got there safe."

"I will." Jade hugged her brother. "I promise."

"Eventually, you're going to have to learn that

I can take care of your sister," Eli joked with Aiden.

"Not happening anytime soon," Aiden said obstinately. "Just call."

I had to bite my lip to keep from smiling. Aiden had been protective of his sisters his entire life. He'd raised them. And he wasn't going to stop just because they were both married now.

There was a flurry of good-byes, and then Aiden and I were finally standing alone in the kitchen.

"I wonder what that was all about?" I pondered. "Jade looked annoyed."

Aiden grinned. "Because her husband almost spoiled a surprise."

I frowned. "What surprise?"

"I'm taking you away for some adult time," he pronounced. "Maya wants to stay with her auntie Brooke at Jade's place for the next five days. Brooke, Liam, and Seth are taking her to the zoo today. And then they're going to stay with her until we come back. Brooke really wants to get to know her niece before she has to go back to the East Coast, and so does Liam."

"We weren't planning on going anywhere." I was confused.

"No plans necessary. I took care of everything."

"Aiden, what are you talking about?"

He moved over to me and kissed me softly on the lips, momentarily distracting me.

When he was finished, he pulled back and drilled me with a laser-sharp look in his glorious blue eyes. "We're taking a break, Skye. Just you and me. And Liam and Brooke are going to stay in California to babysit their niece for us."

My body ached at the thought of being alone with Aiden. "Where are we going? Am I allowed to ask?"

"Nope." He slapped me on the ass. "Go pack your suitcase. We're out of here in an hour."

The mystery and the excitement of the unknown had really piqued my interest.

It felt good to happily anticipate what Aiden had in store. So good that I didn't even remind him that he hadn't exactly asked me to go. But it *was* apparently a surprise.

I'd discovered that I really did like that hint of mischief and mystery in Aiden's eyes. It sparked a curiosity that I nearly couldn't contain.

I went and packed my suitcase.

CHAPTER 18
Aiden

I was relieved when Skye hadn't asked a single question about where we were going.

But not for the reason most people might think.

I was fucking ecstatic that she was comfortable enough to just agree to go anywhere with me.

She was starting to trust me, to feel safe with me.

And I swore I was never going to give her any reason to doubt me.

My bag was already packed and in the truck, so I made myself some coffee and leaned against the counter, waiting for Skye as I drank it.

I loved my daughter with all my heart, but I needed some alone time with Skye so I could figure out how I could banish the hint of sadness I always saw in her eyes.

Even when she was smiling or laughing, that wary uneasiness was still there, and so was that touch of sorrow on her face.

The only time she was ever completely unguarded was when she was with our daughter.

I wanted to hear about her experience of living with the mob. Yet I also wanted to hear *nothing more* about it at all.

I'd probably have nightmares over her being found out and murdered without a second thought by her husband.

Skye had been a possession to Marco, one he could easily give up if it meant saving his ass.

And Skye had probably been in more danger than even she ever recognized.

One slip and it would have been over. One overheard conversation.

Fuck! I need to stop obsessing over the fact that she could be dead!

But my need to protect both her and my daughter wouldn't let my brain rest.

I wasn't even going to try to pretend that I didn't want or need Skye. As far as romantic relationships were concerned, I'd had none except for her.

I'd fucked.

I'd had dinner and dates with plenty of females.

But none of them had ever been Skye. And that was my problem. No matter what had happened, my goddamn heart had never let go of Skye Weston, and most likely never would.

Don't push too hard.

I shook my head at that random thought.

How could I not when I *had* to make her mine? I wouldn't be happy until she had my ring on her finger, and both she and Maya were officially Sinclairs.

Oh, hell, who was I kidding? If I *had* to wait, I

would. I'd already been waiting for her for nine years, even though I'd never recognized it until recently. Maybe patience wasn't exactly one of my virtues—not that I had very many anyway. But if she needed time, I'd try like hell to give it to her.

Not because I wanted Maya as my daughter full time.

Not because I wanted us all to be a family, even though I wanted that, too.

Selfishly, I wanted *Skye* because my stubborn heart had never really let her go. There was no closure to be found for us because I'd finally admitted to myself that there was nobody else for me but her.

I'd either be happy because she was mine.

Or miserable because she wasn't.

I might have been hurt and pissed off for the last nine years, but I'd held on to all the young love we'd had back then.

Yeah, we'd both grown up. But somehow, the woman she was today had only strengthened my resolve.

She was strong.

She was independent.

She was definitely resourceful and smart.

And I wanted her even more than I had when we were barely grown.

"Dad! Hey, Dad!" Maya bellowed as she came down the stairs.

I caught her up as she ran to me, and I hugged her hard.

This kid was still a miracle to me.

Mine and Skye's.

And I'd learned so damn easily to love her more than I loved myself.

"Hey what?" I asked as I rested her on my hip.

"I get to stay with Aunt Brooke and Uncle Liam while you're gone with Mom. They're taking me to the zoo today. And Uncle Seth is coming, too."

"I know. They're pretty excited," I explained. "Your aunt Brooke wants to do things with you before she has to go back to the East Coast."

Maya let out a little-girl sigh. "I love having family. And I have so much of it now. I love Aunt Brooke, Uncle Liam, and Uncle Seth. They're super cool."

I smirked. "Because they let you eat cookies right before dinner?"

Brooke had given Maya a plate of cookies at the reception, and then Skye had wondered why our kid hadn't eaten her dinner. But I had known why. I probably should have told Maya's mother about the cookies, but I hadn't. Aunts were allowed to spoil their nieces once in a while. And Brooke and Liam would be headed back to the East Coast soon, so it wouldn't happen often.

My daughter looked at me earnestly. "Not just that, Dad. I think they really care about me like family should."

My chest ached because Maya had been deprived of family for so long. "They do," I assured her. "All of your new family does."

"Where are you taking Mom?" she asked. "She never gets to go anywhere."

"It's a surprise," I explained. "And I'm trying to take care of the problem of her not going anywhere. Even grownups need a break once in a while."

"Do you think it will make her happy?"

It nearly killed me that even my daughter had been able to sense some of her mother's past trauma.

I nodded. "I hope so, Princess."

"She's getting better now. But she used to be sad. She tried to hide it, but I could tell. Mom tried to do everything to make me happy, but I always knew something was wrong when we lived with Marco."

Out of the mouths of babes.

Maybe it was just an observation, but Maya couldn't be more spot on with her simplistic theories.

I bounced her up and then caught her again, making her squeal like the child she was. "I promise I'll do everything in my power to make you *both* happy from now on," I vowed.

She shrugged her small shoulders. "I'm already happy. I have you and all the rest of my family. Really, I was never unhappy. I just wanted to go and do more things when I was younger, but Mom was always a good mother."

"Was she?" I asked.

My daughter nodded. "The best."

It was pretty amazing how well Skye really had shielded Maya from everything ugly when her daughter was younger. She didn't hesitate to love or trust. Maybe she had sensed that something bad was happening, but she'd never been caught in the middle of any of that. If Maya had any issues, she wouldn't have been able to accept people into her life so readily.

"So you don't mind that we're going to take separate little vacations once in a while?" I asked Maya.

"Nope!" she said immediately. "Can I tell you a secret?"

I nodded, hoping it was nothing bad.

"I hope you and Mom decide to get married. I know you don't have to for us to be a family. But it would be so cool," she said hopefully. "Then we could all be Sinclairs."

"Do you want my last name?" I asked huskily. "Do you want to be a Sinclair?"

She thought for a moment before she said, "Only if Mom does, too. I have Mom's last name, and I don't want to hurt her feelings."

Maya's comment made me more proud than it hurt that she didn't automatically want to be a Sinclair. It told me how loyal she was to her mother, how much she loved the woman who had raised her alone for so long.

"Then I guess I'll just have to convince you both to change your names," I said as I grinned at her.

"I just really want us all to be happy," Maya answered.

I hugged her close. "I want that, too, Princess. Very much."

"You seem a little sad, too," she observed. "Not like Mom, but kind of not totally happy, either."

Damned if my kid wasn't completely in tune and sensitive to other people's moods. I wasn't sure if that was good or bad.

"I'm happy that I have you," I told her.

"But you want us to be a family, too, I think."

"I think you're right, smarty-pants," I said as I tickled her.

"Dad, stop!" she said with a giggle.

"Stopping," I promised as I quickly moved my hand.

Note to self: my daughter can only take so much tickling.

"Can I come here while you're gone to play the new piano?" she asked hesitantly.

"Of course, Princess. This is your home. I'll make sure you have a key in your backpack."

Maya had been diligent about playing the piano every day between her lessons, and I wasn't just being a proud father when I said she was talented.

It hadn't taken her long to pick up the basics, and she was now working on full songs.

Yeah. Maybe I *had* said that I wasn't going to teach her, but I was right there with her every time she practiced to answer whatever questions I could for her.

I tried hard not to be an overprotective, indulgent father, but it was difficult not to want to make up for some of the time I'd missed in her life.

"Thanks," she said with relief. "Someday, I want to play as good as you do, and as good as Uncle Seth plays the guitar."

"Keep practicing and you'll be better than we are," I assured her.

"Mom says that I get all of my musical talent from the Sinclairs, because she can't even hold a tune," Maya mentioned.

A female voice came from near the stairs. "I think somebody is telling all my secrets," Skye said as she breezed into the kitchen.

"Nah," Maya denied. "It's just nonsecret stuff."

I put my daughter down as Skye handed Maya her backpack.

"You should have everything you need in there for several days," Skye told her. "Be good for your aunt Brooke and Uncle Liam, okay?"

"I will. I hope you have as much fun as I'm going to," Maya said confidently.

"She definitely will," I said, my voice husky.

I stared directly into Skye's beautiful green eyes. The glint of fear was still there, but she did smile. And that excited grin slammed me in the chest like a hard swing from a baseball bat.

I guessed a smile would work . . . for now.

CHAPTER 19
Skye

"You have a private jet?" I asked with surprise as Aiden took the road to the airport.

"We all got the idea from Eli," he answered. "That guy has more planes than United Airlines. So Noah, Seth, and I all pitched in and we share one. It's technically the Sinclair jet. I can't say we've used it much, but it's going to come in handy right now. And it will help when Seth and I have to travel more in the future. He has visions of going international, and knowing Seth, I'm sure he will. And I'll have to travel occasionally to meet with sources."

I was so excited to learn what we were doing, but I was curious about what he was envisioning for his future, too. "Do you think you'll have to travel a lot?"

"In the beginning, yeah. First, I need to get the processing facilities built, but then I will need to set up people and places around the world to source the seafood we can't bring in here."

"Any regrets about dropping out of Sinclair Properties?"

He shook his head. "None. And I don't think

Seth cares, either. He's already counting the money he'll bring in from *both* businesses."

"I'm glad you could come to an agreement. I never wanted me or Maya to be the cause of your rift."

"You weren't," he denied. "It had more to do with the fact that he had no right to try to run my life and decide what I should and shouldn't do."

"He was trying to protect you."

"I get that," Aiden answered. "But he went too damn far."

"You don't regret hitting him?"

"Hell, no. He deserved it," Aiden grumbled. "There were way too many really bad consequences because of what he did."

"In the end, taking that letter might have saved your life, Aiden. So I don't regret that he burned it. Had you come after me, you could be dead right now. I had no idea what Marco was when I went with him. In the beginning, I wanted you to come. But later, I was glad you didn't. You would have come in blind, with no idea of what you were up against. Sometimes things just do work out for the best."

"Yeah, but what about you?" he said gutturally.

I shrugged. "I would have preferred it if I had just found another way out, no matter how hard it could have been. But I'm here. I'm alive. And I'm free now. So I still think it happened the way it was supposed to happen, no matter how much

I hate it. Taking them down when they'd hurt and killed so many people was necessary. So will you tell me where we're going now?"

I wanted to change the subject. I didn't want to spoil the trip or the excitement I was feeling over traveling somewhere.

He grinned. "We're taking a flight."

I let out an exasperated sigh. "Obviously. For me, that's kind of exciting. I've only flown once in my life. When I was twelve. My mother took me to my aunt's funeral in Dallas."

He parked the car in the airport parking lot, hopped out, and grabbed both of our bags. "You ready?"

I was already out of the car. "Yes."

He nodded toward the terminal.

Citrus Beach didn't have a very big airport. I was willing to bet that the largest planes that came in and out were probably Eli's and the Sinclair jet.

I scrambled after him, still wondering where he was taking me.

My ex-husband had acquired a lot of money. I could even say that he had been wealthy—though all the money had been dirty.

But Marco's money didn't even begin to compare to the Sinclair fortune.

"This is incredible," I murmured as I ran a hand over the butter-soft leather of the jet's seats.

I finally sat down next to the window, since I knew we were getting ready to take off, and Aiden plopped down next to me.

"Honestly, it still pretty much blows me away, too," he admitted in a deep voice. "I guess I'm not used to owning stuff like this. Hell, I had my doubts whether I'd even be able to own my own house, much less a beachside mansion."

He put his seat belt on and then reached over to fasten mine.

"What does it feel like to go from being poor to having more money than anybody could ever spend in a lifetime? It's not even like winning the lottery, because the Sinclair fortune is so vast."

I knew that Jade had experienced some difficulties adjusting to having so much money. I had no doubt it had affected all of them in some way or another.

"Hell, even after all this time, I still think that there could have been some kind of mistake," he confessed. "I was a blue-collar guy trying to eke out a living to keep my family above water. For a while, I couldn't touch the money, even though Evan called it our legal inheritance. It didn't feel like it was mine. It took me a while to really connect myself with all that money. Sometimes it still feels weird. But having that much money has its perks. You're in one of them right now."

"But the money was as much yours as it was Evan's and his family's on the East Coast.

You had the same father, but none of the same advantages growing up," I reminded him.

"In some ways, I'm grateful that we were the bastard family," he admitted. "Evan, his brothers, and his sister didn't have a very good childhood. Our father was a mean son of a bitch. We probably got out lucky since we hardly ever saw him. My family might have been poor, but we were all there for each other, and we knew that Noah loved us all enough to fight for us to stay together when our mother died."

"So when did you figure out that it *really was* your money? That it really was an inheritance you deserved?" I questioned.

He turned his head and grinned. "I'll let you know. I'm not totally sure I'm there yet. But at least I've learned to spend it like it's mine."

The aircraft pulled into position for takeoff, and I grabbed Aiden's hand.

He squeezed it. "Nervous?" he asked.

I swallowed hard. "A little. But I'm excited, too. I don't remember much of my flight when I was a kid."

"Just try to relax and enjoy the speed," he said as he threaded his fingers through mine.

The jet took off like a shot, and my heart soared right along with the engines.

I was almost disappointed when we lifted off the runway and I couldn't feel the acceleration anymore.

"I never knew I was an adrenaline junkie," I said with a laugh. "But that was fun."

"Not completely true," he drawled. "I distinctly remember a time when it used to turn you on that we might get caught screwing in the great outdoors."

Heat flooded to my core. "I did not love that," I denied. "I was just happy to be with you."

Part of me knew I was lying. Although everything about the Marino family had terrified the hell out of me, playing with *Aiden had been* exhilarating. That tiny element of danger that we might get caught in the park in the dead of night had added a little to the frantic pleasure he'd always given me.

"Deny it all you want, sweetheart. But you were pretty damn wet when I used to warn you that we could get caught," he reminded me.

"Okay," I said in a *whoosh*. "Maybe a tiny part of me liked it a little."

Really, what I'd *loved* was having him inside me.

The profound connection.

The passion.

The abandon I'd felt when he had me all worked up.

With Aiden, sex had been new and exciting in *every way*.

"It seems like the sun is behind us. Are we headed east?"

"Pretty much," he said. "Do you remember telling me how much you wanted to see Las Vegas when you finally hit drinking age?"

My heart lifted. "Yes! Is that where we're going?"

I'd always wanted to go to Vegas. I'd wanted to see the bright lights and craziness of the city.

"We'll be there shortly," he said with a boyish grin. "And there's nothing we can't do there. I would have picked something more exotic, but Vegas is close, and I knew you weren't going to want to be away from Maya more than a few days."

"No. It's perfect, Aiden. Oh, my God. I can't believe we're just flying to Las Vegas to have fun."

Taking off to a party place on a whim wasn't even something that had ever occurred to me, much less something I'd think could happen for real.

I was a struggling single mom, and women like me didn't get a chance to do these things.

Usually.

I leaned over, put an arm around his shoulders, and kissed him because I couldn't help myself, taking my time to savor the taste of him before I finally pulled back. "Thank you for this. It's the sweetest thing anybody has ever done for me."

My eyes started to tear up, but I blinked hard until they dried up.

Don't cry. You can't cry.

"I wasn't doing it to be sweet," he said warmly. "Maybe I'm just trying to get laid without our daughter around."

I snorted. Aiden was incredibly sweet, whether he wanted to admit it or not. "This will definitely get you laid as many times as you want, any way that you want," I teased.

He tipped my chin up, and he kissed me this time.

And his embrace was rough, but tender.

I sighed into his mouth, and he explored for so long that I lost track of anything except his lips on mine.

He was demanding, but the kiss was still sweet.

As he pulled back and looked into my eyes, he growled. "Be careful what you promise, sweetheart. I've been deprived for a long time. You might never see Vegas."

My body was already primed from his uncomplicated but fierce embrace. "I'm starting to think that wouldn't be so bad. We could always come back," I said breathlessly.

I'd quite happily spend several days naked in a hotel room with him. I had no doubt that I wasn't going to be happy to see him get dressed, either.

"We have to eat," he mentioned.

"Room service?" I suggested.

I'd been so hungry for Aiden. I always had been, even when I hadn't liked him very much.

202

The two of us had a primal, elemental attraction that gnawed at me unceasingly, and it was making me crazy.

He stroked a hand over my hair. "I've got plans for us, Skye, but I left a lot of downtime."

"Thank God," I answered, and then dived in for another kiss.

CHAPTER 20
Aiden

"You're good, sweetheart. Tuck your cards," I told Skye as I sat next to her at a blackjack table.

She turned her head and looked at me, her eyes shining with mischief. "How do you figure that out so fast? And how do you know I should stay with what I have? I've only got fourteen. Shouldn't I take a card?"

I shook my head and adjusted myself on my stool again.

One smile, one look, and my dick was harder than a rock.

The woman was killing me, and she didn't even know it.

"It's all about the odds. He has a card up that, according to the odds, should make him bust. It doesn't always work that way, but you have to follow the same odds all the time."

She smiled brighter. "Okay, that makes sense."

Skye had pretty much been elated since we'd come into the hotel. Probably way earlier than that, if I wanted to count her joy at flying in an airplane—and I *was* counting that, because I treasured every damn moment that she was happy.

She'd laughed like a carefree girl through dinner, and then again when we'd tried the slot machines. Playing cards wasn't her thing, but she'd been game to try it.

The waitress dropped off our drinks, and I tipped her as I watched the game play out.

The dealer busted.

"I won," she said, sounding delighted.

I'd won, too, but I wasn't looking at my chips.

I couldn't take my eyes off Skye.

In her black cocktail dress and ballbuster high heels, she was every man's fantasy.

Her blonde hair had been pulled up into a large silver clip, but tendrils had escaped throughout the night, a look that made her even more desirable.

Hell, I was pretty sure she could wear a burlap sack and my dick would find her irresistible.

"Are you okay?" she asked in a concerned tone.

She'd obviously just noticed that I was staring at her. "I'm good. I guess I got distracted."

"Do you want to take a walk?" she suggested.

I nodded, not trusting myself to speak. If I did, I'd be telling her exactly what I really wanted.

A walk would be good.

I needed time to try to pull my shit together.

I put my chips into my pants pocket, and I watched her as she carefully placed hers in a tiny black purse that she secured over her body with a long strap.

We grabbed our drinks—since we'd asked for plastic to-go cups, there was no problem carrying them out of the casino.

"Where to?"

I took her hand and led her outside, knowing she'd love the lights now that it was completely dark.

"Let's just stroll down the Strip," I advised.

Since it was still spring, it wasn't ungodly hot.

We walked aimlessly, not caring where we were going. It didn't matter to me as long as Skye was with me.

"If I haven't said it already, thank you for this," she said softly after several minutes had passed. "It's incredible. And the lights are amazing."

"I was pretty sure you'd like it," I said with a smirk. "And stop thanking me. I'm enjoying this, too. I haven't been to Vegas for years. It feels good to take a break."

"I can't remember when I've been this relaxed," she agreed as she sipped her drink. "Of course, it could be the alcohol I've consumed, too."

"Two glasses of wine at dinner and the drink you have now are not going to get you drunk."

"I don't want to get hammered," she shared. "I want to remember every minute of this. Have you noticed that there's art everywhere here? Sculptures, paintings, and amazing photographs. It's pretty spectacular."

Now that I thought about it, she was right. It

wasn't something I was looking for, since I didn't know shit about art. But it was the kind of thing that Skye would notice. "Vegas is over-the-top in almost every way."

"Maybe that's why it's so much fun," she considered.

"Speaking of Vegas insanity, did you want to ride any of the things you saw online?"

She'd been on the Internet moments after I'd told her we were going to Vegas. I'd loved watching her point out all the attractions in the city.

"The Stratosphere coaster for sure," she said excitedly. "Honestly, I'd love to do any of them."

That's my girl.

Skye had always been pretty much fearless. So I wasn't all that surprised that she wanted to try anything and everything.

"We'll check it all out tomorrow," I promised. "Maybe catch a show tomorrow night."

She let out a happy sigh. "That would be amazing. I've never seen a live performance."

She sounded so ecstatic that my erect dick was twitching. I wanted to pin her against a wall and capture that happiness while I pounded myself into her until the unrelenting desire I was feeling right now was satisfied.

I tossed my drink back in two gulps and then dumped my cup, hoping the alcohol would calm my ass down.

We walked the Strip for quite some distance, watching the Bellagio fountain show and other activities happening as we strolled and stopped.

As we were headed back to the hotel, Skye commented, "Sometimes I feel like being here with you is surreal. So much time has passed, and so many things have happened. But the feelings are the same."

My heart almost jumped out of my chest. Skye had told me she loved me back then. Was *that* still the same?

"Is that good or bad?" I questioned.

She sucked up the last of her drink, and my eyes stayed riveted to those rosy lips that I wanted to be wrapped around my dick.

Skye tossed her empty cup in the trash. "Maybe a little bit of both. I'm different now, Aiden. You know that. I don't trust easily, and I'm not open about my emotions."

"Give it time, sweetheart. You need to *learn* to trust me."

"I do in here." She put her hand to her chest. "But my head screws with me sometimes."

Hell, I'd take that. Eventually, her mind would catch up with her heart and instinct.

"You went through hell, baby. Give yourself a break and just let it happen naturally."

"My body has changed, too," she said with a sigh. "I'm not eighteen anymore, Aiden. I have stretch marks and a huge old scar from my

C-section. Plus, a couple of pounds of belly weight that I could never get rid of."

I turned my head to look at her. "And you think that's going to be a problem for me at all? Oh, hell no. That's a major turn-on."

She had my kid, and she'd have the marks from that forever. How could I not find that pretty damn hot? Well, not the fact that she'd suffered—alone—bringing our daughter into the world. But seeing the signs that she'd carried my child was going to be an aphrodisiac for me—not that I needed any more of those right now.

Skye slapped me on the arm playfully. "You're being absurd," she said with a nervous laugh.

"I'm being totally honest," I grumbled.

We entered the casino and headed toward the elevator. I'd seen Skye yawn several times, and it had been a long day.

"Ready to go up?"

She nodded because the casino was noisy.

When we got into the elevator, everything was silent because it was a semiprivate lift that went up to the penthouses.

She leaned against the back wall and stared at me with curiosity. "Are you serious about the stretch marks and the scar? Because they aren't pretty. Neither is the baby weight I've never been able to get off my belly."

I punched the button up to the top floor and then turned to her. "Let's just get this out of the way. Let me see them," I demanded, my cock as hard as a giant diamond.

Reaching out, I caught the skirt of her above-the-knee cocktail dress and started to haul it up.

"What are you doing?" she said with a laugh as she tried to slap my hand away.

I kept lifting. "Checking out those unsightly scars you think are ugly."

I sucked in a swift breath once I had the dress up to her breasts.

Not only could I see the marks from childbirth, but Skye was wearing nothing but thigh-high stockings and a tiny thong underneath the lightweight garment.

"*Jesus Christ, woman!* Are you trying to kill me?" I growled and dropped to my knees.

"Stop, Aiden. We're in an elevator." Her tone was half-amused, half-mortified.

"I want to see these scars up close," I mumbled as I buried my face in the soft skin of her stomach. "They look pretty damn hot to me."

"Get up," she said with a giggle.

I ignored her and ran my lips over the few faint stretch marks, and then traced the C-section scar with my tongue.

"Totally erotic," I said, my voice muffled from having my face against her skin.

It was silky and warm.

Skye was beautiful everywhere, and if she was

carrying any extra weight, it was all in the right places.

"We're stopping!" Skye sounded panicked as she tried to smooth her dress down.

I got up and dropped the hem right before the doors opened.

I took her hand and squeezed it as an older couple entered the semiprivate elevator.

Her cheeks were adorably red, and Skye was flustered as she shot me an admonishing look.

But she was still smiling.

And we both laughed once we were free of the elevator and back in the penthouse.

CHAPTER 21
Skye

"They could have seen you on your knees and under my dress," I told him as he locked the door of our suite behind us.

I was trying desperately to be serious.

However, I knew I'd given myself away by laughing through what should have been a reprimand. But I couldn't help myself. Honestly, I knew that Aiden would never expose me to anyone. Still, he'd cut it pretty damn close.

Aiden *had* accomplished one thing, though. He'd taken away all of the nervousness of revealing my changed body to him. And now all I wanted was to get *him* naked.

God, I needed him so desperately that I could hardly stand it.

Heat had flooded my pussy when he'd lifted my dress. Not that I hadn't been ogling him all night, and thinking about both of us being naked, hot, and entwined.

I'd just been slightly apprehensive about revealing my body. It wasn't the body of an eighteen-year-old anymore.

I'd been through childbirth, which had taken its toll.

He pinned me against the wall, his big body heated against mine. "Why didn't you tell me you were wearing almost nothing under that dress? Your ass is bare."

I wasn't really into thong panties. But . . . "I wore them for you. You didn't have to know until it was time for you to find out."

"Good thing I didn't know," he rumbled. "We never would have left this damn room."

There was no comment about my changed body. While it *was* hard to believe that my scars actually turned him on, I didn't think he was bothered by them, either. He seemed even more obsessed with my sexy underwear.

He buried his face in my hair. "Jesus, you smell so damn good. Like strawberries."

I smiled. "It's just a body spray. I'm not really into heavy perfume."

"It's sexy as hell," he growled as he pulled back to look at me. "Everything about you makes me crazy, Skye."

I could feel how aroused he was when he ground his hips against my pelvis. "I want you, Aiden. So badly that I can't stand it," I told him honestly as I met his gaze.

I wasn't going to hide the way I felt anymore. I was just as needy as he was . . . Maybe more. "I need to feel you. I need you to fuck me."

His eyes erupted with molten heat. "You need me to make you come," he stated.

I nodded jerkily. "Please. I feel like it's been forever."

He buried his hands in my hair, and then lowered his head, his mouth covering mine with a force that I welcomed.

There was nothing subtle about my attraction to Aiden.

It had always been all-consuming.

I moaned against his lips, savoring the feel and the taste of his marauding embrace.

I was panting as he finally pulled back and then dropped to his knees.

"You've already seen the scars," I whimpered. "Please."

I was more than ready to beg him to fuck me. I needed him inside me.

My body trembled as I squirmed when his tongue started tracing my scars again, but I jumped as one powerful jerk divested me of my panties.

I nearly went up in flames as I realized that he planned on putting his mouth somewhere else, and he wasn't shy as he dived into my slick pussy.

The first touch of his tongue probing at my slit sent me reeling, and I let out a moan of pleasure that I'd never heard come from my lips before.

This was new.

It was foreign.

And it was so damn hot that I felt swept away to another place, another time.

It was a promise he'd never had the time to realize.

He'd always talked about how much he wanted to taste me, years ago, but our couplings had been quick and basic, from necessity.

My ex-husband had been nothing but brutal, and his face had never gotten anywhere near that area of my anatomy.

But Aiden was there now, and apparently loving every minute of it.

I parted my legs a little more to give him better access.

And when he finally buried his face completely into my quivering pussy, I literally screamed because the pleasure was so intense.

He tasted me like a man who had been deprived of sustenance way too long. Like he was famished, and I was his only source to feed on.

"Oh, God. Aiden," I groaned.

A million sensations exploded from my body, and the way he made me feel was almost frightening.

But I was more desperate than I was afraid.

"More," I pleaded. "Please."

He gave me more when his slick tongue slid over my clit.

And then he took it away when he licked me from bottom to top.

"Aiden. I need to come. Please."

The heat and pressure building up inside my core was intense. I had to have relief.

I felt greedy, and completely lost. I speared my hands into his hair, and pulled his face flush against my vulnerable pussy.

I needed . . .

More pressure.

More heat so I could burn hotter until I orgasmed.

More of . . . Aiden.

"Yes," I screamed as I felt the pressure of my climax building.

I leaned my head back against the wall and closed my eyes, my pleasure so powerful that I could barely stand.

His large hands cupped my ass tightly, but I didn't care. It felt good to have his fingers clutching me like he never wanted to move from where he was right now.

He used his grip to pull me onto his face harder. The pressure and the feel of his tongue teasing my clit were nearly unbearable.

I fisted his hair as I felt the first powerful waves of my orgasm completely consume me.

I had no control; I was along for the ride.

Aiden was lapping at my juices that flooded my core as I experienced a climax so strong that it rocked me, and it was the most erotic thing I'd ever heard. He kept sucking like he had to have every bit of me, even as my climax became merely ripples, and then just an overall sensation of floating.

I yanked on his hair. "Fuck me," I demanded.

I was single-minded. I had to feel him inside me, even though he'd just given me one of the most powerful orgasms I'd ever experienced.

He came to his feet and I let go of his hair, the wild look in his eyes so fierce that my core clenched in reaction.

He yanked his sweater off, and I salivated as I saw all that smooth skin pulled tight over toned muscles.

I wanted to touch him, but I wanted him naked even more.

His shoes, socks, pants, and boxer briefs all came off in a frenzy.

I yanked my dress over my head and then removed my bra.

When we were joined, I needed it to be flesh to flesh.

"I can't wait any longer, Skye," he growled as his naked body pinned me against the wall.

"Don't, then. Fuck me right now," I answered as I panted with anticipation.

I'd caught a brief glimpse of his enormous hard cock, and I wanted to claim it. I wanted Aiden inside me.

"Wrap those sexy legs around my waist," he demanded as he lifted me up by my ass.

I had no sooner obeyed him than he plunged inside me desperately.

Bam!

My rear end hit the wall, his hands cushioning the blow.

And then he was there, inside me, around me, consuming me.

I strained against him, needing every inch of his cock, even though he was already stretching me.

"Ride this with me, baby," he rasped next to my head. "Stay with me."

Like I could do anything else?

And then it hit me that he didn't want me to be afraid. That he knew that sometimes I had flashbacks.

"I'm not thinking of anything else but you," I said breathlessly. "Just fuck me, Aiden. I need you."

"Jesus Christ! I need you, too, Skye. So damn much," he said with a ferociousness I hadn't heard from him in years. "Always have. Always will."

I tightened my legs around his waist, encouraging him to move. "Then take me."

My body never did and never would belong to anybody but him.

He pulled almost out of me, and then slammed back in. "You were meant to be mine," he snarled. "You and me. We were always right."

"I know," I panted.

His fingers pressed into the skin of my ass possessively as he started to set a frenetic rhythm that made me spin out of control.

I was *free* when I was with Aiden.

I was *wild* when I was with Aiden.

I was *me again* when I was with Aiden.

No holding back.

I rode his cock as he pummeled inside me.

Harder and harder.

Faster and faster.

Until our bodies were slick with sweat.

When he started grinding against me with every hard entry, I felt like I was spiraling out of control.

I wanted that stimulation to my clit every time he filled me.

"Yes. I need to come," I screamed.

"I'll make you come," he rasped.

He drove into me deeper, and at an angle that rubbed against my clit so hard that I exploded.

"Aiden," I yelled as my body imploded.

"That's it. Come for me, Skye. I can't wait any longer."

It became obvious moments later that I was coming. I scratched at his back and bit down on his shoulder, because I didn't quite know how to handle the extreme force of my climax.

Aiden's body tightened, and he groaned my name, "Skye. Baby. Holy hell."

His big body shuddered, and he found his own heated release deep inside me.

There was nothing but the sound of our labored breathing as we recovered. I was too stunned to speak for at least a couple of minutes.

"Goddamn it to hell," he finally said as he put his forehead on my shoulder.

I stroked his sweat-slick back. "What?"

"I swore we were going to do it in a bed the first time."

It took me a minute to realize that we'd never found ourselves in a bed together, even though we'd had sex.

And we hadn't made it to a bedroom this time, either.

I didn't care. I had no control when it came to the man who was frustrated because he didn't think we'd done it quite right for the first time in almost a decade.

I couldn't help myself.

I laughed.

CHAPTER 22
Skye

We never made it to a bed the second time, either.

Aiden and I had decided we both needed a shower, and after we'd explored each other's bodies in the multiple sprays from the fancy shower, we hadn't bothered trying to get to the bedroom.

"We finally made it," I teased as I looked at all the room-service items that were spread out on the bed.

Both of us had experienced midnight hunger pangs, so we'd ordered up some food.

Funny that we were eating on the bed we'd wanted to fuck on.

He grabbed a couple of fries, dunked them in ketchup, and then dropped them into his mouth before he said, "About damn time."

I smiled as I took a bite of my burger. I was sitting cross-legged and naked on the bedspread, while Aiden was sprawled out beside most of the food.

I'd gotten over my nervousness about my changed body, and I had no qualms about sitting in front of Aiden naked now. Honestly, I was starting to believe that I turned him on just the way I was.

All I could really think about was that it was a darn good thing that we had a king-sized bed to accommodate all the food we'd ordered.

"Are you complaining?" I joked.

He caught my gaze and slowly shook his head. "Never. It doesn't really matter to me. I just thought you needed to experience taking it slow in a damn bed for once."

I snickered. "I don't think we know how to take it slow. And it doesn't matter to me, either."

"You do realize that we didn't even think about protection," he finally said. "You're the only woman who has ever made me forget about that."

"You're safe. I'm clean. And I still take birth-control pills."

"No worries here, either," he admitted. "I've been checked, and I haven't been with somebody else in a long time. And never without a condom."

We ate in silence for a couple of minutes before he asked, "How do you want it, Skye? Tell me what really turns you on. What are your fantasies?"

How could I tell him that every naughty fantasy I'd ever had was about him? And that it didn't much matter how we got to the hot and sweaty parts.

I shrugged. "I don't think I really have any except for being nailed by you. Positions are optional. I just don't like it doggie style. Or . . . anal."

He must have heard the trepidation in my voice, because he nailed me with a sharp look. "Why? Did he hurt you?"

I'd polished off my cheeseburger, and I wiped my hands with the napkin. "You know he did."

"With anal?"

I nodded slowly. I was done with not telling Aiden everything. We were having a sexual relationship. He deserved to know. "Yes. It hurt. I think he liked that. He always pushed me down on the bed face-first, and then did it that way."

His expression turned thunderous. "You can't just do it. Granted, it's never been a big thing for me, but you need lube, and to take it slow. Work into it over time."

"That's never the way it happened," I said with a shudder.

"Is that why you never got pregnant again?" he asked in a softer tone.

"God, no. He was an equal-opportunity abuser. That was just his preference a lot of the time. I took my birth control like clockwork. I hid them so he didn't know. The last thing I wanted was to get pregnant with his child."

"You know I'd like to kill that bastard?" he asked.

I shook my head. "Don't. Don't hate him. He's not worth it. None of them are worth it."

I'd learned a long time ago to not give Marco the power to make me feel anything, even hate.

He didn't deserve any emotions from me. I couldn't help the lingering PTSD that I had, but I refused to consciously let myself feel anything about the criminals I'd helped put away. They'd taken up enough of my life.

"Maybe not," he grunted. "But *you're* worth it. I hate him and every bad thing he ever did to you. But the bastard is in jail, so I can't kill him."

"I wouldn't let you even if he wasn't," I said softly. "Then I'd lose you."

I could see the tension in Aiden's muscles release. "I'm not going anywhere," he rumbled.

At that moment, I wanted to move across the bed, climb inside his gorgeous, naked form, and stay there for the rest of my life.

For the first time in a long time, I felt . . . safe. And I knew Aiden made me feel that way.

"You know I'd never hurt you, right?" he asked.

I popped a fried mushroom in my mouth and chewed as his laser-sharp gaze was trained on me.

"I'm not afraid of you, Aiden. I never have been. Maybe I was worried when I found out that you didn't know about Maya, but I've never felt a single twinge of fear that you'd physically hurt me."

"I didn't mean to mentally hurt you, either," he said in a powerful voice.

"I know. If I hurt you, it was unintentional, too," I told him honestly.

He lay back on the pillow, obviously done with the food. "Do you want to know the truth?"

"I do," I encouraged.

"You broke my heart when you left. Maybe we never talked about a future because I knew you had schooling you wanted to do, and you were so young. But even then, I wanted to marry you, Skye. I knew it wasn't happening for years. And that was okay—I was willing to wait because you were still too young."

My heart tripped, and then it started to throb.

He'd known years ago that he wanted to be with me?

Aiden had never told me that he loved me, but thinking back, he'd *shown* me that he did. Even though we didn't talk about a serious future together, we'd planned all the things we'd wanted to do as a couple. So what if we hadn't talked marriage? He'd let me know he was coming back, and that he considered us a couple. Sometimes actions mattered more than the words.

"I'm sorry I hurt you," I said, my voice trembling with emotion.

"I really never got over you," he continued. "It took me several years to even go on casual dates again. And it was never the same because those women weren't you."

"I never got over you, either," I confessed.

"Then why did you brush me off when you first got back to Citrus Beach?"

"I wasn't ready to talk. I was still angry that you hadn't come after me, even though I was glad you didn't because you could have ended up dead. Really, I was the most upset because you didn't recognize or care about our daughter."

"But I didn't know about Maya," he pointed out.

"I didn't know that."

"I have to admit that it still hurts that you'd think I'd ever brush off you and my child," he said huskily.

"Then I'll tell you that I was sad you'd ever think I'd just up and leave you because of money. I would have rather been poor with you than to be with a guy just because he was rich. I didn't care about Marco's money. Honestly, I never saw much of it anyway. I didn't want to touch it."

"I get that now," he replied. "I was stupid."

My lips curled into a small smile. "I was an idiot, too. But I'm glad you're here now."

"And I'm rich now, too," he joked.

"Do you really think I care about that?" I asked. "I mean, it's nice that you don't have to struggle, and that you're finally going to have your own business. But money doesn't mean that much to me, Aiden. It never has."

"For me, having the money is still new. But it *does* mean that I can make sure you and Maya always have everything you want and need."

He sat up and reached for something on the

side table. "Which reminds me that I got you something."

"You already gave me this trip, Aiden, you don't need to buy me things—"

"I wanted you to have it. When I was browsing down at the shops, I had to buy it. It reminds me of you."

My hand trembled as I took the oblong box. "What is it?"

He grinned. "Open it. It's not really a big deal."

I shot him a skeptical glance. Everything nice Aiden did for me was a big deal. Maybe he didn't recognize that, but nobody had ever cared enough about me to think of giving me a gift. The only one I'd ever gotten was his mother's necklace, and that piece of jewelry meant everything to me.

Carefully, I pulled the top off the box, and I knew immediately why he'd purchased the contents.

I carefully lifted the delicate bracelet from its nest of soft cotton and rubbed it with my fingers.

"It matches the necklace," I said in an awed tone.

"Not exactly," he corrected. "There are differences, but they could be a set. It's meant to be on your wrist. I knew it the moment I saw it."

"I've never seen anything so beautiful," I said in a breathy voice.

The bracelet had the same vintage look as the necklace did, and every stone was like a duplicate of the one on the only piece of jewelry I had.

Even now, when I was sitting around naked, I could still feel the cool gold of the delicate chain against my skin. I rarely took the gift Aiden had given me off my body. It had been like a talisman to remind me that life wasn't always as bad as it had been with the organized-crime family.

The necklace had seen me through some pretty hard times.

"I've never seen someone more beautiful than you are. The bracelet belongs on your wrist. Just like the necklace should always be next to your skin," Aiden said gruffly.

He was staring directly at me.

And I felt like something had finally shifted inside me.

His gift was always going to remind me that even when we weren't together, he was thinking of me, wondering what I'd like or dislike.

It would make me feel like there was never going to be a time when Aiden wasn't thinking about me and our child.

I released a small sigh.

Aiden was the best man I'd ever known, which was probably why I'd fallen head over heels in love with him all over again.

Or maybe I'd never *stopped loving him*.

"I love it so much," I said as I handed it to him to put on my wrist. "Thank you."

He secured the clip in record time, considering

how big his fingers were and how delicate the catch had to be.

He nodded when he was done. "It was definitely made for you."

I looked at the bracelet, and then I did something I hadn't done in many, many years.

A single tear dropped onto my cheek.

And then another.

I made no attempt to blink them back or stop them. There was no ceasing it this time.

Before I knew it, I was being held against Aiden's shoulder.

The man I was in love with had forced me into the world of feeling my emotions again.

For the first time in a long time, I cried.

CHAPTER 23
Aiden

I wasn't sure whether I should be alarmed or glad that Skye had finally lost it and gotten in touch with her emotions.

All I could do was hold her tightly while she bawled like the entire world was ending.

I *wanted* her to feel alive again, to feel like it was okay to emotionally express herself.

But I sure as hell didn't like the fact that she was crying.

It broke my goddamn heart.

Even though I knew it wasn't sorrow she was feeling.

"Everything will be okay, baby. I promise," I vowed to her.

"I know," she said tearfully. "I'm not sad. I'm happy. Sometimes you're just so sweet."

I flinched because what guy wanted to be considered *sweet*, really?

Honestly, I'd much rather be her stud.

Picking up the bracelet had been an impulse. It matched the necklace that she already had so well that she just had to have it. And it wasn't like I was the least bit short on funds.

For me, the bracelet had been a trinket and

nothing more. It reminded me of the necklace, and I had hoped it would make her smile.

But holy shit! I had never expected all hell to break loose over it.

To make her stop crying, I said, "I'm an asshole, too, sometimes. Remember?"

She made a sound somewhere between a laugh and a sob as she pulled back and met my eyes.

And then she smiled, and looked at me like I could fly.

I thanked whatever instinct had led me to that bracelet and given Skye back to me. Hell, I'd even be *sweet* if that's really what she wanted. Or I'd at least try.

I gently swiped the tears from her cheeks. "Okay?" I asked.

She nodded vigorously. "Definitely okay."

I got my buck-naked ass off the bed, moved all the trays and plates to the dresser, and then pulled her underneath the covers with me.

All I really wanted was to hold her, and make her realize that there was never going to be a day when I wasn't going to be around for her from now on.

Now that the dam had broken on her emotions, I needed her to know they were safe with me.

Skye and Maya were my whole damn world, and somehow I wanted her to *feel that*.

"You're always going to be safe with me, Skye," I said in a husky voice I nearly didn't recognize as I pulled her soft body against mine.

I was determined to make up for every single day she suffered at the hands of a madman because my brother had screwed things up for both of us.

"I know that," she said in a sleepy voice. "I won't promise you that I'll never have an episode or flashbacks. But it's never because of you."

"I'm not exactly a snowflake, baby," I answered. "I can take whatever happens. I just want you to feel like you're safe."

"I do. Best feeling in the world," she murmured. "I guess when you go years feeling scared, you appreciate not having to look over your shoulder in case somebody wants to kill you."

"Were you still doing that? Even after it was all over and everyone was in prison?" I questioned.

She buried her face in my chest. "Sometimes I do. But not so much anymore. Old habits are hard to break. It's like my inability to let myself cry or let anybody know what I'm feeling. Any weakness was always used against me, Aiden. It's hard to shuck that defense mechanism, even when I don't need it anymore."

I understood that in a twisted kind of way. I'd spent my entire life watching every single cent I earned. And I still caught myself wondering if I could afford something before I remembered that I had money. Some things got ingrained into the brain, and it wasn't easy to change those habits.

Except spending money wouldn't kill me. So Skye's habits had to be a lot harder to change.

"What's on the schedule for tomorrow?" she queried.

I knew she was trying to change the subject, and I wasn't about to push her any more tonight. "Whatever you want. This is your trip."

"But I want you to have fun, too," she insisted.

I'd been inside her body.

And I'd fucked her until she was screaming my name.

Anything else that happened besides being able to touch her was pretty damn unimportant.

"We can go ride the rides around town if you want," I said. "Or go downtown to check it out. There's also the option of taking a trip to the Hoover Dam, or seeing one of the shows. You tell me what *you* want to do, because I'm already happy," I said.

"I'd really love to ride the observation wheel," she said longingly.

"Done," I agreed. "But that won't take all day."

She rubbed her sweet body against me, and she let out something like a purr as she said, "I'm not so sure we'll get out of here *that early*."

Holy hell. I wouldn't argue if she wanted to stay in the entire day and night, but I had noticed in the shower that she was sore. So I had to make my dick behave.

"I can tell you're hurting," I said sternly.

"But it hurts so good," she said seductively.

I put my thigh gently between her legs, and then wrapped my arms around her waist. "Go to sleep or you'll get more than you bargained for," I cautioned her.

I didn't need much rest between one time and the next. Not with her. My dick was ready to go within minutes when I was with her.

But I didn't want my pleasure in exchange for her pain.

I gave her a playful pat on the ass. "Go. To. Sleep."

I only had so much restraint.

"Did I already thank you for the bracelet and for this trip?" she asked quietly.

Her words were muffled against my chest.

She *had* thanked me. About a *million times*. "You did."

"Well, then, thanks one more time. I think I really needed this. Maybe I just needed some time away from California."

I'd never really thought about the fact that she was still living pretty close to where bad things had happened to her, and it wasn't unusual to have to make a trip from Citrus Beach to San Diego. Even though the coastal city was growing, there were still certain attractions you just couldn't find there.

It had never occurred to me that maybe she needed to leave, start a new life somewhere else.

"We could move," I offered. "Start someplace else."

I was a billionaire. Hell, anything was possible. We could move to the Caribbean if that's what would help her forget the shit that had happened to her in Cali.

"I thought about that," she admitted. "But I'd still be running away."

"It's not unreasonable to not want to live in the same state where you went through hell."

"But I don't really want to move, Aiden. I like my life in Citrus Beach. You have your family there, and I have my friends. The restaurant and your new business, too."

"I'll get my own damn jet, and we can travel back and forth."

"Not necessary," she said firmly. "Marco isn't even in prison there. They transferred him and most of the family to a supermax prison in Colorado. And I figured out that moving wouldn't make me happy. Why should I leave a place I love because I had some bad memories close by? They'll fade away with time. Especially now that I have so many things to replace them with."

That made sense. "Okay. If you want to stay."

"I do. All things considered, I'm not leaving Citrus Beach. I grew up there. I have a lot of good memories with Jade, and even you, there."

"Like the park?" I asked playfully.

Every sexual encounter we'd ever had when we were young had been at that city park.

My daughter had been conceived there, and now we took her there to ride the swings and play on the teeter-totters with her friends.

"One of my favorite places," she confirmed as she rubbed her head against my shoulder like she was getting comfortable.

"I know you didn't have it easy, sweetheart, but it was a good place to grow up."

"Other than my crazy mother, I loved it," she agreed.

I suddenly wondered about a detail we'd never discussed. "What did your mother know about Marino?"

"I'm not sure," she said uncertainly. "I think she knew that his fake religious agency was actually a front to lure women and underage girls and boys into human trafficking. I don't know how she couldn't have known. But I'm pretty sure she was brainwashed into thinking that she was saving their souls in some way. She was crazy, Aiden. But I never saw her involved in any of the other crimes that I was informing the FBI on."

"You didn't talk about any of that with her?" I pretty much knew the answer, since Skye had never had a mother she could trust.

"I didn't dare," she uttered. "Even if she wasn't involved, I wasn't going to convince her that I was right and the Marino family was evil."

"When did she die?"

"About six months before the FBI did their raid and arrested everyone. I'm not quite sure that she wouldn't have been implicated if she'd lived. Maybe she was nuts, but she was breaking the law and aiding the Marino family in their human-trafficking ring. Whether she was aware of it being evil or not."

I put my face in her hair because I was addicted to her scent. "I'm so damn sorry that nobody has ever been there for you."

I'd had a whole damn family of people to back me up whenever I needed it. Skye had never had anybody she could trust. Not even her mother.

"I had Jade," she protested. "I didn't talk to her much while I was married because I couldn't. And I would have never wanted her to know what was happening, because that knowledge could have put her life in danger. But she's always cared. She was and is the best friend a woman could have."

"You have me now, too."

"I know. It isn't the quantity of people who care, you know. It's the quality," she said earnestly.

I chuckled. "And you think Jade and I are quality?"

"Definitely."

"You do realize that all the rest of my family is going to get to know you, and they'll be there for you, too?"

"I think I could handle that," she said, her voice slightly fading.

I kissed her on the forehead and closed my eyes because I knew she was falling asleep.

It was reassuring to know that if anything ever happened to me, my family would take care of Maya and Skye in a heartbeat.

Good to know that having a shit ton of brothers, sisters, and cousins wasn't *always* a pain in the ass.

CHAPTER 24
Skye

I was just a little melancholy when I woke up on our last full day in Vegas.

Every moment I'd spent with Aiden had been a gift for me.

I could feel myself finally changing, metamorphosing into the woman I wanted to be.

Yeah, I felt a little raw because I wasn't used to my emotions being close to the surface. And just a little bit apprehensive. But those feelings were fading fast.

I'd rather be a woman who cries and feels genuine joy than one who's like an emotional vacuum.

And the man who had brought me on this trip had been the catalyst I'd needed to come out of my shell of protection and start really living again.

Aiden made me feel safe.

He made me feel adored.

And he made me feel like the most fascinating, beautiful woman he'd ever encountered.

That attention was heady, and it had gotten to me.

Him buying me that bracelet had been my

tipping point, the moment when I just couldn't contain what I was feeling anymore. And I hadn't regretted it for even a second.

The last four days had been heaven, because I'd been able to truly experience every emotion while we were together.

We'd visited every crazy ride and roller coaster in Vegas. Then, he'd surprised me with a helicopter ride over the city and Hoover Dam.

Last night we'd gone to a hilarious comedy show.

The days had flown by, much to my dismay.

Today was our last day. We'd take off tomorrow for home.

We hadn't made any big plans, but I was all for playing slot machines and then visiting the ginormous swimming pool at our hotel for a while before dinner.

"What are you doing, beautiful?" Aiden asked as he walked into the big living room the suite provided.

I looked up at him from my spot on the couch. "Thinking about how sad I'll be to leave. It's been an amazing few days. I think I'm completely spoiled."

He winked at me, which made my heart skitter. "You deserve it. This was a really short trip, though."

"I'm okay with going back. I miss Maya."

I'd talked to my daughter every night, but

FaceTiming her wasn't the same as hugging her good night.

"Me, too," he admitted gruffly.

"So are we ready to head downstairs?" I hopped up from my seat.

He wrapped his arms around my waist, and I leaned in to fill my lungs with his scent.

Aiden smelled like fresh air, sandalwood, and a little bit of mint, and it was a fragrance that always came to mind every time I thought about him. His scent was unique, and so damn addictive that I wanted to stay right where I was.

"So you're ready to tackle the slot machines?" he said with a hint of mischief in his tone.

"I am. We haven't really spent all that much time in the casino. I was hoping we could hit the pool later. I need some exercise. I've been eating like a pig."

Sex seemed to be an appetite inducer for me. I'd been stuffing my face with every type of food I could get since we'd arrived in the city.

"That's one of the attractions in Vegas. Food," he joked. "And you're not in any danger of putting on any pounds. We've been working out every night."

I snorted because what he said was true. We'd been practicing our bed aerobics every single night. "Not enough," I told him.

No matter how much I'd loved every touch, there was no way it had burned off all the calories in the rich desserts and other decadent food I'd been eating.

"I'd be more than glad to give you more," he rasped into my ear.

His hands cupped my ass and squeezed the cheeks through the pair of shorts I was wearing.

My body caught fire as he put a hand on my back and plunged his other one into my hair.

I opened my mouth just in time for him to cover it with his own.

And just like that, I was primed and ready.

That's all it took with Aiden. One touch, and I was aching for him to fuck me.

I wrapped my arms around his neck and strained to get closer to him, my already-hard nipples abrading his chest as I started to squirm.

He gave me no mercy, and I wanted none.

I gave and he took my mouth like he couldn't get enough. He nibbled my lips as we caught our breath, and then he swooped in again.

"Aiden," I panted when he finally left my mouth and started tasting the sensitive skin of my neck.

He nipped at my earlobe. "Tell me what you want, Skye."

"You," I whispered. "I just want you."

"You have me, sweetheart," he said huskily against my ear. "You'll *always* have me."

He reached for the bottom of my tank and

pulled it skillfully over my head. "You're so damn beautiful, Skye."

Our clothes came off in a frenzy of activity, both of us working to get the other one naked.

When we'd finally achieved our goal, we just stared at one another, our breathing ragged with desire.

I couldn't keep my eyes off Aiden's nude form, the perfection of his body as he stood in front of me without a hint of unease.

I'd gotten used to him staring at me with no clothes on. Any modesty I'd had was gone.

But I was still speechless when I saw him nude, and he wasn't the least bit hesitant to get himself as naked as the day he was born.

My breath caught as he moved forward slightly and cupped my breasts, his thumbs aimlessly caressing my pebbled nipples.

"Perfect," he pronounced.

Heat rushed between my thighs, followed by a flood of warm moisture. I leaned against the desk chair behind me, and let my head fall back. "Aiden," I said with an aroused sigh. "I need you."

"How much do you need me?" he said gruffly.

I whimpered as he lightly bit my nipple, and then soothed it with his tongue.

"Bad," I answered with a groan. "Really bad."

Every sexual desire in my body had come roaring to life the moment he'd kissed me like it was as necessary to him as food and water.

He pulled me toward him, and then turned me around so I was facing the mirror on the large desk before he wrapped his arms around me from behind.

"Watch me, Skye."

I met his gaze in the reflection, and my stare didn't waver.

Slowly, he placed my hands on the desk until I was bent over. "Are you okay with this?" he asked hoarsely, his eyes burning into mine.

I could see him.

I could feel him.

How could I *not* be okay with it?

And then it hit me exactly *what* he was trying to do.

I hated sex from behind.

But there wasn't any part of me that was hesitant as long as I could see him.

I slowly nodded as I maintained my bent-over position. "Yes. I'm better than okay."

He was trying to erase the bad memories for me, and I was going to try my best to let him do it.

He moved behind me and fondled the cheeks of my ass, his gaze never wavering from mine.

Nudging my legs apart, he delved into the quivering pink flesh of my pussy, and I almost forgot to breathe. "Yes," I hissed. "Please."

"You're so damn wet for me, sweetheart," he growled as his fingers sought and found my clit.

"I want my cock buried so damn deep inside you that I never want to come out again."

He stroked over the tiny bundle of nerves, his expression intense.

I bit my lip as he stroked harder over my slick clit, pushing me higher. After several days of being together, he knew every button to push to make me come so hard that I saw stars.

I lowered my head to the desk because I couldn't hold it up anymore. My body was screaming with a longing that went so deep that I didn't feel like I could hold it up.

"Don't," Aiden commanded. "Don't stop looking at me."

He grasped a big lock of my hair and gently pulled to urge me to watch him.

He wants me to know who I'm with. He doesn't want me to forget that it's he who's taking me from behind.

If it was at all possible, that made me want him to come inside me even more.

I wasn't afraid; I needed *him*.

Some of my hair was in my eyes, but I could still see his muscular form as he gripped my hips and surged forward with so much power that I would have stumbled forward and hit the floor had I not been able to steady myself on the desk.

Our eyes were locked as he started to hammer into me from behind.

It wasn't the most intimate position, but it was

hot as hell. Being this way with him felt different. Deeper. Harder.

I started meeting him stroke for stroke, pushing back as he pushed forward, and I could feel and hear our skin slapping together erotically.

"More," I demanded as I pushed my hips back.

I wanted him so desperately that my body wouldn't be satisfied unless I could feel every thrust.

And I did as he stopped holding back and gave me the ferocity I had to have.

I closed my eyes as he drove into me with a power that was mind-blowing, and at an unceasing pace that shouldn't have been possible.

"Yes, Aiden. Yes," I screamed, not caring if people could hear me.

I was close. So close. And all I wanted was to come.

The moment he reached down with one of his hands and found my clit, I lost it. My climax happened fast and furious.

Aiden found his own release immediately after I did, and he held my shaking body up even as he orgasmed.

He buried his face in my neck, and we stayed like that, neither one of us moving, and the only sound in the suite was our heavy breathing.

My entire body was quivering, and I couldn't have done without the support of that desk for a minute or two.

He picked me up and collapsed with my body on top of him onto the couch.

I knew I had to be squashing him, but he wasn't complaining.

It took a few more minutes for my heart to stop galloping and my breathing to finally slow down.

"I'll never look at doggie style quite the same way again," I told him as I was still struggling a little to catch my breath.

I heard him chuckle as I slid to his side, my leg still slung over his supine body, his arms still tightly around me.

"That wasn't truly doggie style," he said playfully.

"Then I'll be happy to let you tutor me in that, too."

I was completely convinced that I was never going to forget who I was with when it was Aiden. The feel of him, and the pleasure he could give me, was way too powerful to be mistaken for anything else.

I love you. I love you so much.

I wanted to say the words so badly that it was physically painful to hold them back.

But we hadn't talked about love.

And I wasn't sure it was something he was ready to hear.

We were still trying to work out our future together.

I jumped when his hand connected with the cheek of my ass.

"Don't fall asleep," he warned. "We have slot machines to conquer this morning."

I laughed. "What if I said I was way more interested in exploring doggie style than the slots?"

"I'd say that we'll get to them later," he said eagerly.

I nipped at his ear before I replied, "I think we should *definitely* get to them *later*."

He shot off the couch and picked me up. I wrapped my arms around his neck to steady my body.

"Like after lunch or something?" he suggested.

"Or something," I agreed.

I didn't care whether or not we *ever* saw the slot machines.

Not when I could have Aiden all to myself.

We ended up skipping the slots, and didn't surface until dinnertime.

Best. Day. Ever.

CHAPTER 25
Aiden

It took me two weeks after we got back from Vegas to admit to myself that even if it took forever, I'd wait until Skye was damn good and ready to marry me.

Sure, it was what I wanted, and like any stubborn guy, I wanted to get my way.

I'd had a very nice diamond burning a hole in my pocket for over a week now.

And I still hadn't popped the question.

Truth was, I needed her to want to be committed to me just as much as I wanted her to have everything I had to give.

I wanted her to trust me completely. And, hell, I couldn't blame her for being slow to trust anyone after what she'd been through.

Until I could *feel* that she was ready, just being with her was enough.

I'd finally realized that marriage was just a piece of paper. What really mattered was our relationship with each other.

Marriage wasn't going to keep her from leaving again.

That job was all on me. And I didn't plan on screwing it up.

The last few weeks I'd felt like me, Skye, and Maya *were a family*.

I didn't have to have a piece of paper to prove it.

I wandered out to the kitchen, missing Skye's presence because she'd gone to pick up Maya from school.

She'd only been gone fifteen minutes, and I was already missing her.

It was getting way too natural to be able to wander in and out of her home office all day, since hers was right next to mine.

She'd spent a lot of time helping me out. Skye had strengths in areas I didn't, especially organization. And she'd been invaluable at helping me get all my ducks in a row.

Construction was starting soon on a processing facility right outside of town, and I'd already purchased a couple of fishing boats. I was on track to get my business up and running on a reasonable schedule.

I grinned as I saw the sandwich Skye had made me sitting on the kitchen counter.

Every day it was another creation.

And every single day, she came up with something better than the day before.

That was one of the amazing things about Skye. She wasn't a quitter, and she didn't settle for mediocre. She kept trying to outdo herself, come up with something even better, even though what she'd done the day before had been pretty damn good.

Her plan to make the restaurant into an upscale deli was a pretty damn brilliant idea. People headed to the beach in the summer could take stuff to go, but there would still be a nice seating area for patrons to relax, sit down, and have themselves a great lunch or dinner if they weren't in a hurry to get to the beach.

I looked at the handwritten note she'd left beside the plated sandwich:

Hawaiian pizza grilled-cheese sandwich with dipping sauce. Make sure you use the sauce. It makes it taste better.

I had no idea what was in the concoction, but the toasted Italian bread looked pretty damn good.

I picked it up and took a bite. I could taste the pineapple, but the cheese and ham were front and center.

As usual, it was better than the one I'd tried out yesterday, and I hadn't thought she'd be able to top the apple barbecue pulled pork.

I dipped it in the sauce, and then discovered in the next bite that it was even better with marinara. I should have taken her advice the first time.

The plate was empty within a few minutes, and I put it in the dishwasher, congratulating myself again for getting the job of official taste tester for the menu Skye was working on.

It was kind of ridiculous that she actually thought that eating her creations was some kind of help to her, or any sort of sacrifice on my part.

It was an occupation I thoroughly enjoyed.

Another winner, sweetheart.

That sandwich *definitely* needed to stay on the menu. Right alongside the five other ones I'd sampled in the last five days.

I was going through the mail that Hastings had dropped off at the house when my daughter and her mom came through the door.

"So, what did you think?" she asked immediately.

Maya ran toward me like a runaway train, and I scooped her up and told Skye, "The best one yet."

She rolled her eyes. "You always say that."

"Because it's true. You outdo yourself every single day. Your deli is going to be a huge hit."

She beamed at me. "I hope so. *You* should hope so, too, since we're partners."

I didn't want to burst her bubble by reminding her that I could well afford the loss if the place didn't fly. The success of her new restaurant was something I desperately wanted to see because it was important *to her*.

Honestly, I knew it would be a success, because Skye didn't know the meaning of failure. She'd bust her ass until the place was running exactly the way she wanted it.

At some point, I knew I'd end up calling her on working too much. But for now, she was sticking to our bargain of knocking off at a reasonable time so we could spend our evenings with Maya.

My daughter hugged me, kissed my cheek, and then politely asked me to put her down because she wanted to go practice her piano.

I watched her scamper away, and I put my arms around Skye. "Everything is going to be fine. Don't drive yourself crazy. You have a great design for the new place, and I guarantee the menu will be very well received. It's unique and different."

She put her arms around my neck and kissed me before she answered, "I hope so. I guess I could have just redecorated and reopened, but I really think the café *needed* a change. It was outdated in more than just the décor. The menu was stale and old. This is a beach town. People are looking for something unique, something that stands out."

"You needed to make it into something that was really you. I know it's been in the family for a while, but there's no reason why it can't change to be something you want."

She nodded. "It's stayed the same for way too long. How are things going for you?"

"Great," I said. "Construction will start on time. And I already have some boats purchased. They'll be delivered next week. I'll have to work on getting some sources for the stuff I can't get here. But I have time. I'm not expecting this to get built up overnight. When Eli gets back, I'll pick his brain for some advice."

"They'll be back on Saturday," she reminded me. "It seems like Jade has been gone forever."

I nodded. "I agree. I'll be happy to see Eli, too. Maybe he can help me out a little with the business side of this new venture. I know the operational part of it, but not the details of the actual business side."

"It's got to feel crazy sometimes, right?" she asked. "I mean, you used to fish for other people, and now you're doing a start-up yourself."

Honestly, it was unreal. Had somebody told me a few years ago that I'd end up a billionaire who was trying to build my own giant seafood company, I would have told them that they were out of their mind.

But it was happening. "Sometimes, I still don't believe it," I shared with her. "How does a poor guy like me end up with a life like this?"

"But you've worked hard your entire life, Aiden. If anybody deserves this life, it's you."

"Plenty of people work hard, and they don't become this rich," I grumbled. "In fact, there's very few people in the entire world as rich as we are. And the vast majority of them were born into some money."

"They didn't work like you did. You sacrificed everything to keep your family together."

"So did the rest of my family."

She smiled at me. "I rest my case. They're all loaded now, too."

I grinned back at her. "Smartass."

I reluctantly let her go as she went to pick up Maya's backpack and school stuff to put away.

I went back to sifting through mail while she left the room to put things away in Maya's bedroom.

I tossed most of the stuff I'd gotten into the trash. Since I'd purchased an expensive house, I got offers for everything from mortgages to credit cards.

Why did it seem like the entire world knew I was now incredibly rich?

One interesting thing about being wealthy was that I sure as hell got a lot of mail.

A year or two ago, I was worrying about having enough money to buy groceries.

And now I got preapproved offers for an endless amount of high-limit credit cards, mortgages, and lines of credit—like I needed *that*.

Pretty crazy for a guy who only knew how to fish for a living.

I kept trashing things until I got to the bottom of the pile.

The last piece of mail caught my attention because it was about something I'd pretty much forgotten about.

Maya and I had taken a paternity test soon after

Skye had informed me that Maya was mine.

Now, it seemed like we'd done that ages ago.

It had become so unimportant that I hadn't even thought about the test until I saw the reminder just now.

I went to toss it into the trash, unopened.

Maya *was* my daughter.

I had no doubt about that, and neither did any of my family. She looked just like Brooke and Jade when they were little.

And she looked like . . . me.

My offspring had me tied around her little finger, but I was pretty sure she didn't know that she did, because she was such a good kid. I'd been blessed with the best child ever. Hell, she even had manners, but that was something I could thank Skye for. She hadn't learned those from me.

I wasn't sure how it had happened, but I'd gotten so accustomed to being her father that I couldn't imagine a life without Maya and Skye anymore. So many little things had made us all close.

The family dinners with just the three of us.

Getting Harry Potter read to me and Skye every night.

Maya's warm hugs that made me feel like the luckiest dad in the world.

Our weekends, and planning fun things to fill every Saturday and Sunday.

It was almost unbelievable that the two of them hadn't always been here, because I felt like we'd been together forever.

They were my whole damn world now.

I didn't need proof from some damn laboratory to tell me that Maya was my daughter. She *had been* from the first moment I'd seen her.

But for some reason, I hesitated instead of trashing the results.

I'd paid for it. I should at least read what the lab had to say, right?

I was pretty sure that I couldn't get rid of it without reading it, because unopened and unread mail had gotten me into so much damn trouble in the past.

Skye's letter.

Not reading that had changed the entire course of my life.

I wasn't a superstitious type of guy, but I tore open the envelope anyway.

I was pretty fucking happy, so I decided to just read the results instead of pissing off the gods of fate *just in case* they existed.

I was way too happy to push my luck in any way.

There was a lot of medical jargon that I really didn't understand all that well, so I kept shuffling through the lab results until I could come across something I could comprehend and be done with it.

There was something called a combined paternity index.

And probability of paternity.

A data table of DNA markers.

Lastly, there was a conclusion.

There was one line I understood perfectly, and it stopped me in my tracks.

I was *excluded* as Maya's biological father.

I kept reading that line over and over, like it was going to magically change.

Not possible. There's no way.

Much as I tried, I couldn't make those words change, so I started trying to process a truth I just couldn't accept, even though the scientific data was right in front of my eyes.

The child I'd already come to love and adore *was not* my daughter.

CHAPTER 26
Skye

"I'm starving. I thought we'd just throw some burgers on the grill, and I'll make some potato salad," I told Aiden as I went back into the kitchen. "Sound okay to you?"

I went and pulled the burgers out of the fridge, and Aiden still hadn't answered, even though he was standing right behind me.

I dropped the meat in the sink and turned.

He was obviously in the same space that I was.

But his mind was completely somewhere else.

His body looked tense, his palms braced on the counter, and his head was down, staring at something I didn't recognize.

"Aiden, are you okay?" I said, concerned.

He didn't answer.

My first worry was that it was bad news about somebody in his large family.

"Aiden," I said louder. "You're scaring me. What's wrong?"

When he finally turned his head, his beautiful blue eyes were cold, and that terrified me because I'd never seen his expression so glacial.

"Tell me what's wrong," I implored.

"When were you planning on telling me that

259

Maya isn't really my biological child?" he said in a guttural voice.

I moved to him and put a hand on his bicep, because I had no idea what he was trying to say, but I wanted the furious, chilly, and confused look on his face to ease.

I needed him to talk to me, because what he was asking didn't make sense.

"What are you saying?" I asked quietly.

He jerked his arm away from my hand. "I'm saying that I got the lab results on the paternity test. I'm excluded as her biological father. *Excluded.* Zero chance of Maya being my child."

"That's crazy. It's not even possible," I told him as I reached toward the counter and snatched up the lab results.

I was silent for a moment as I read through all the technical stuff, but I quickly dropped to the bottom of the last page to see the conclusion.

What I saw stunned me as much as it probably had Aiden. I had to read the line a couple of times just to make sure I was interpreting it correctly.

He was right.

He *was* excluded as Maya's biological father, which was conclusive proof that she wasn't biologically his child.

"This isn't right, Aiden. It has to be a mistake," I said in a horrified tone.

He looked at me with a laser-sharp, thunderously pissed-off glance. "Is it? Or was I just a good target to be the dad since I'm now rich, and conveniently here in Citrus Beach?"

I felt like he'd just slapped me. *Hard.* And he hadn't even touched me.

"That hurts," I told him in a tremulous voice.

"Yeah. Well, *it hurts* to know I love Maya like she's my child, and she's not. Never was, according to the DNA test. And DNA doesn't lie, Skye. Just tell me why the hell you did it. Why you made all this up. Was it the money? Because that's the only thing that's really changed about me."

"I didn't make it up. And it was never about the money. I told you that," I said flatly. "I swear."

I couldn't completely blame him for being upset, but he *had* to know that Maya *was* really his daughter. He had to. Maybe it *was* hard to go against a DNA test, but in *his heart* he had to realize the truth.

Problem was, he was thinking completely with his brain right now, and he was right, lab tests rarely lied.

People did.

So he'd immediately jumped to the obvious conclusion right away. And what in the hell could I say in my defense except the truth? Which probably *would* seem highly unlikely to him right now.

"Since her birthday is in May, you must have forgotten about me pretty damn quickly. Or is she really Marino's kid?" he asked angrily.

I took a deep breath and tried not to let my

temper fly, too. That wasn't going to help the situation right now. "I would have never been with him if it wasn't for Maya. You know that, Aiden. I told you that I was pregnant with her when I agreed to go with him because I had nowhere else to go."

"Bullshit!" he said in a frustrated voice as he took back the lab results and held them up. "Are you trying to say I should believe you and not the test? I might be gullible when it comes to you, but I'm not stupid."

He'd *never* been gullible or stupid, but now probably wasn't the time to try to convince him of that.

Honestly, I wasn't sure what had happened, or why we'd gotten the wrong result. But I did know the truth, something that he definitely didn't want to hear right now.

"All I can say is that it's a mistake," I said softly. "I don't know what happened, but you know I wasn't with anybody before you, and I sure as hell wasn't with anybody soon after. We need to call the lab."

His expression was tormented. "Do you know how many guys probably do that, just fucking hoping the test was wrong?"

I got that he was angry, but I refused to let him keep using me as a verbal punching bag. He'd hate himself for it later, because that was just how Aiden was made.

I put my hands on my hips. "It is wrong. There's no question about that. The only answer I need is how it got screwed up."

"I can't do this anymore, Skye," he said as he dropped the papers on the counter.

He didn't say another word as he walked to the garage and left.

A few moments later, I heard the sound of the garage door opening and closing, and then the engine noise of his truck fading away.

I took a deep breath, and then let it out. Tears leaked from my eyes. The pain of all he'd said was gut wrenching. Yeah, I understood that he might be justified in his anger, but it killed me that he hadn't even listened, or considered the fact that it could have been a mistake.

Damn emotions. I was better off when I couldn't let them come to the surface.

Now that I had, I was pretty much screwed.

The pain of watching Aiden walk away was almost more than I could bear.

I picked up the papers and looked for contact information.

They close at five p.m.

There was no way I was going to get any answers tonight.

And what would happen if they told me that there was no mistake?

I knew better, but Aiden didn't.

And I had no idea if I could eventually talk

him into doing the test again with a different lab.

"Mom, did Dad just leave? I saw his truck from the window of the music room," my daughter asked anxiously as she came into the kitchen.

I swiped at my tears before I turned to her. "He did. But I'm sure he'll be back."

Eventually.

At the moment, there was no reasoning with him.

"Why did he go? It's time for dinner."

I smiled at her. "Dinner is coming up. I was going to make hamburgers. Do you want to go hang out at Aunt Jade's place to make them? I have a key."

My best friend had told me to feel free to use her place anytime while she was gone. And I was going to take her up on her offer. I really didn't want to be around to fight with Aiden when he came back. I was pretty certain he wasn't going to just blow off steam that easily.

His heart was understandably broken because he thought his daughter really wasn't his blood. And nothing I could do right now would convince him that she was.

"Why would we want to go there? Dad's house is nicer."

Good Lord! Nobody had ever told me how to explain fights to an eight-year-old. And the situation was so much different from when she'd only had a stepfamily that constantly ignored her.

But I never lied to Maya. Okay, maybe just a little about Santa Claus and the Easter Bunny, but she was getting old enough that she knew the truth about those things anyway.

"Something . . . happened. And your dad is a little upset with me. But he'll get over it. He got some bad information. That's all. I don't blame him for being angry, but I can't get the right information until tomorrow." That should work, right? I wasn't blaming Aiden or saying anything bad about him.

"Mom, you can just say that you and Dad had a fight. My friends' parents fight all the time. I think it's kind of normal."

I frowned at her. "Do you think so?"

She shrugged. "When you love somebody, they can still make you mad, right? My friends say their parents get upset about money sometimes, or other stupid stuff."

I watched as she climbed up on a stool at the breakfast bar. Her eyes were nearly level with mine, and she didn't look all that concerned.

"It *was* kind of ridiculous, but I think he needs some time to come to his senses," I explained, marveling over the fact that sometimes kids could simplify things that seemed pretty complicated to adults.

She nodded. "Then we can go to Aunt Jade's. It would be fun. But can we come back here tomorrow? I think we'll both miss Dad."

I was teary-eyed. My daughter was right. We were both going to be missing Aiden. I could only hope that he didn't push Maya out of his life before he had confirmation that she really was his daughter.

"I don't know. We'll see what your dad says, okay?"

There was no way in hell I was going to let my daughter know that her father had questioned whether or not he was her biological father. It would crush her if she thought he was rejecting her in any way.

"He won't stay mad," she said reasonably. "He never does."

"That's because you've never given him a reason to be all that angry at you. You're a good girl, Sugar Bug."

She might be curious and inquisitive, but my daughter was far from being a brat. I rarely had to set my foot down with her, and Aiden was so patient that I doubted she'd ever seen her father this ticked off. Which was another reason it was better if I stayed at Jade's for now.

Maya idolized Aiden.

And I wanted it to stay that way.

"Should I get my backpack?" she asked.

I nodded. "Put some clothes for school in it, and everything you need for tomorrow."

I'd figure out the details later. Aiden and I would have to talk to each other eventually.

The lab was actually close. I'd go to San Diego after Maya went to school if I needed to, and find out how and why the results had been screwed up.

And I knew they had.

I'd been with two men in my life.

Aiden.

And I'd endured the rapes my husband had dished out.

So I had no doubt who the father was, since I'd been pregnant before I'd even considered taking Marco up on his offer of marriage.

My chest ached for the pain Aiden had to be going through at the moment.

Maybe it was hard to believe *me* when the DNA results had been right there in front of him.

But it still destroyed me that he had doubted me, even when he had good reason to be skeptical.

I only wished that he could have listened to his heart.

CHAPTER 27
Aiden

"Please don't tell me that you think, for even a second, that Maya isn't really your daughter," Seth drawled as he handed me a beer and then dropped onto his sofa with his own bottle.

When I'd left my house, I'd had no idea where I was going. For some reason that I was currently questioning, I'd headed down the beach to my brother's place.

No matter how pissed off I may have been with Seth, I'd always shared stuff with him, and it had been my natural instinct to show up on his doorstep.

My head was still reeling from the lab results. I hadn't thought it was possible for Skye to lie about something this damn important. Actually, as far as I knew, she wasn't really the type of woman to tell falsehoods at all.

"I'm excluded from being her father, Seth. It's there on the papers. I guess I should have brought them with me for you to see, but you'll just have to believe me. I saw it with my own eyes. Many times. *Excluded* means I can't possibly be her biological father. It's DNA, for fuck's sake. How could it be wrong?"

He shrugged and took a slug from his beer. "Shit happens. Nothing is ever one hundred percent if you have humans doing the work. Think for just a minute, Aiden. Maya is like a mini you. There's no mistaking that she looks just like Brooke and Jade did at her age."

"Coincidence," I grumbled. "All of us are dark haired."

"It's not just *her hair*. It's her facial features, too, and you know it. She's undeniably a Sinclair. Believe me, if I thought she wasn't, I would have told you. But not one of us has ever questioned it, because she looks so much like you."

"Then tell me what the hell you'd think," I demanded. "Wouldn't it have messed with your head, too?"

"Hell, yeah," he answered. "I'd probably believe the test results. But I'm trying to make you calm the hell down and see that even though the possibility is minute, the test *could* be wrong."

"And the chances of that?"

"Slim to none," he answered matter-of-factly. "But it *could* happen. And in this particular case, you should at least think about it, since she bears an uncanny resemblance to a Sinclair."

I tossed my head back and swallowed half of my bottle of beer before I replied, "I already love Maya like she's mine. So what in the hell do I do now?"

"Love isn't about DNA," he remarked with uncharacteristic candor. "I guess I think a kid can still be yours without having your genes."

"I'd still love her just as much," I confessed. "This is more about Skye lying to me in the first place. Hell, she didn't have to. If she'd shown interest when she got back to Citrus Beach, I'd have dated her. Maybe that makes me a fucking idiot, but I could have fallen for both her and Maya once she'd come back home. She didn't have to lie."

"I don't really see her as a user," Seth mused. "All she seems to want is a successful business. And you said yourself that she's been helping you get your shit together for Sinclair Seafood. I'm not defending her, because most likely she did lie. I'm just being honest about what I've seen since you two have gotten together. She's not exactly out spending your money, if that's what she was really after."

And if she'd asked, I would have given it to her. Any damn thing she wanted. But Skye has never even hinted that she wanted money.

That observation made everything just that much more complicated. I had no idea what her motives could have been.

I drained my beer. "She *has* been helping me," I admitted. "And her business ideas for the restaurant are phenomenal. She even insisted we do the partnership paperwork so my investment was safe."

"Hard worker. Honest in business. And a good mother. Does it make sense that she's trying to get something for nothing?" Seth pondered.

"I'll call the lab in the morning," I said flatly. "If I have to, I'll do the test again just to verify the results."

"Maybe the results are true. Then what are you going to do?" he asked.

"I have no goddamn idea," I admitted. "I can't really imagine my life without them anymore. But if I can't trust Skye, I can't be with her. Those lies would destroy me. But it's going to kill me if I don't have any rights to be a father to Maya."

"Maybe she was desperate," Seth suggested. "You did say she had lived in a pretty run-down apartment. What if she just wanted better for her kid?"

"At my expense?" I questioned. "She could have just dated me until I married her."

As crazy as I was about Skye, it wouldn't have taken very long for me to suggest she live with me.

"Most parents would do anything to make sure their children can eat. There wasn't much we weren't willing to do to keep our family together," Seth said.

I thought about his words for a moment. Really, I had to admit that family was a pretty good motivator. I knew what it was like to want something better for my siblings. It was the reason I'd busted my ass to see the younger ones get an education. "She could have asked me for help."

Seth snorted. "After she left you for another guy? I'm pretty sure she wasn't expecting to get a nice, warm welcome."

"I would have helped her," I shared. "I sure as hell wouldn't have let her and her kid starve, even though she did leave me."

"I think you need to prepare yourself for either possibility. One: she lied to you because she was desperate, which is the most likely scenario. Two: somebody messed up on the test results."

I took a deep breath and then let it out. I needed to think rationally. My brother was right about that. But every sensible thought had flown out of my head when I'd looked at those results from the lab. I'd felt like my entire world had just collapsed.

Now, my gut instinct was telling me that Skye wouldn't lie unless she was somehow backed into a corner. And maybe she had been. Yeah, she was living with me, but she had yet to ask me for a penny for anything she personally wanted. Hell, she hadn't even accepted anything for Maya. And if I wanted to get honest, I owed her for years of child support if Maya was my biological child. The only reason I'd never paid her for that was because I was under the impression that I'd always be there to take care of her and Maya.

"It doesn't really matter if Maya doesn't have my DNA," I finally told my brother. "I'd be pretty damn proud to call her my daughter."

"Then talk to Skye and be reasonable," he answered.

I looked at Seth as a light bulb went on in my head. "You like her."

He nodded. "I like her because she makes you happy. And so does Maya. And I already know you're crazy about her. You've never hit me before, even though there were times I might have deserved it. Only a guy who's head over heels does that."

"You really deserved it this time," I grumbled. "And I'm not apologizing."

Seth smirked. "No apologies necessary. Just go patch things up with Skye. Your sad mug is starting to depress me."

It was probably time for me to head home. I'd been gone a couple of hours now, dumping all my bullshit on Seth. "I'll talk to her."

He nodded. "I don't want you to be with somebody who is going to be a habitual liar, or a woman who isn't going to put as much emotional energy into the relationship as you are. But I also don't want you to screw this up twice because you don't have all the facts. Get all the information before you lose it."

Was it possible that Skye was so desperate

that she'd made stuff up just to house Maya somewhere better? To give her daughter a better life? And if she did, could I really blame her?

"She really acted like it was all a mistake," I considered as I stood up. "She looked as surprised as I was."

I was just now getting rational enough to think about *her* reaction. There had been no guilty expression, or any hesitation when she'd said that Maya was most definitely my daughter.

Seth followed me to the door. "Just listen to her, Aiden. Get her side, and follow your gut until you can get a new test done. Until you know the truth, don't do something that can never be undone."

"I plan on it," I answered. "How are things going with the tree hugger who doesn't want you to develop the land on the water?"

"Not good," my brother answered unhappily. "She's taking legal action to stop it. And since she's an attorney, she has connections. And she knows how to write some scathing emails. I hate environmentalists."

I grinned despite my worries because Seth looked so disgruntled. It wasn't often that anybody really annoyed him.

"You don't hate your little sister, and she's a conservationist. And don't voice your opinion to Jade," I cautioned him. "She might punch you in the face, too. You know she'd side with your tree hugger."

"Hopefully this will be over before she gets back," he replied. "Call me tomorrow and let me know how things worked out."

I nodded and walked out the door, suddenly eager to straighten out the mystery of why Skye had lied to me, now that I was thinking straight again.

By the time I arrived home, I was considerably more composed than I had been when I'd left my house.

If I could get the truth from Skye, I was going to listen and put myself in her shoes. I was ready to fight for us if she was ready to never lie to me again.

Dammit! There had to be some compelling reason for her not to be truthful.

And Maya *would* be my daughter. I wasn't all that concerned about whether or not she shared my genes. Seth was right. Love wasn't about DNA. I was pretty sure I already adored her a lot more than her natural father—wherever and whoever the hell he was. If it wasn't Marino, I certainly hadn't seen any other male ready to step up to the plate.

The house was dark, and the first thing I noticed when I pulled into one of the garage stalls was that Skye's beat-up old vehicle was gone.

Where in the hell would she go at this hour?

I glanced at the clock and realized it wasn't

really as late as it felt. For me, it had already been a damn long night. Still, it wasn't like Skye to take off with Maya late on a school night.

I went into the house through the garage and hit the lights.

I heard something I hadn't experienced in a while, and I discovered that I really didn't like the sound.

Everything was dead silent.

I ran up the stairs, taking two at a time, and found Skye's bedroom empty. I went to my room, because more often than not, she slept there since we'd returned from Vegas.

The bed was neatly made, and no Skye.

Hoping she might have fallen asleep in Maya's room, I ran there.

My heart started to race as I found my daughter's room unoccupied, too. The bed was still made and hadn't been slept in at all.

"Dammit," I cursed as I went back downstairs. "Where in the hell is she, and why did she go?"

I'd said some pretty shitty things to her, but I'd never given her a reason to be afraid of a confrontation with me.

But she's never seen me as angry as I was earlier.

And then I saw the note.

There were only four words, scrawled on the back of the paper where she'd written the name of the sandwich I'd tried out earlier in the day:

Maya is your daughter.

She'd left the bracelet I'd given her and my mother's necklace, right next to the note.

I picked them up and toyed with them, noticing that the stones felt cold.

Where in the fuck did she go?

And where in the hell was my daughter?

Did leaving the jewelry mean something? Maybe that she didn't want anything from me?

I placed the bracelet and necklace back on the counter.

I need to find them.

A fierce protectiveness overwhelmed me, made me forget that I was ever angry.

I had no idea where she'd go at a moment's notice. She'd given up her apartment, so maybe a cheap motel?

That thought didn't go over well with me. Granted, Citrus Beach was a small city without a ton of crime, but I didn't want her in a place where she and Maya weren't completely safe.

But since I wasn't sure about her financial situation, it might have been all she could afford.

I kicked myself mentally for never asking Skye if she had enough money in her personal accounts.

She'd never said she was short on funds, but I doubted she ever would. Skye and Maya had been taken care of here, but I had no idea what she had in the bank.

I'd encouraged her to close the restaurant, so it wasn't currently bringing in income. Hadn't been for weeks.

I grabbed my keys, and I was out the door a few seconds later.

CHAPTER 28
Skye

The next morning, it took several cups of coffee to get my eyes completely open.

I'd fed Maya and put her down to sleep early enough the night before. But even though I'd hit the bed not much later, I hadn't been able to sleep.

Around noon, I was still feeling completely exhausted, and more than a little jittery from all the caffeine I'd consumed.

And worst of all . . . I was missing Aiden.

Was I angry that he hadn't listened to me when I'd told him that Maya was his child? *Yes.* I was hurt.

But did I understand his hesitance to accept my word? *Kind of.*

My heart ached, but my brain comprehended exactly *why* he'd been upset.

I just wished he hadn't been so vehemently sure that I'd lied to him. His accusations were what really hurt the most.

I could have understood much easier if he'd just been . . . confused.

He hadn't even had enough time to truly *accept* the fact that he was a father to an eight-year-old,

279

so finding out suddenly that Maya supposedly wasn't his blood had to have been difficult.

Aiden had readily believed me about the letter I'd left him, albeit with Seth's backup of confessing that he'd taken it.

However, it was hard to accept that *science* could actually be wrong.

Really, how well did he know me anymore? We'd had a brief summer love that had ended in disaster. And we'd only been reconnected for a matter of weeks.

Unfortunately, my heart and my body hadn't taken long to come to terms with how I felt about Aiden, but sometimes absolute trust took time.

I hadn't trusted Aiden *immediately*.

And he'd had a load of things he'd taken on that had changed his life.

So rationally . . . I could give him a break.

But that didn't mean that I wasn't sad that he'd refused to listen to the truth.

I got up from the table and went to the kitchen for another coffee. I'd been working on the designs for the new restaurant, and my vision was blurry from lack of sleep.

I'd just have to live with being wound up on caffeine.

I had been trying to work since Maya went off to school, but my brain just wasn't into it.

I knew I was going to have to go talk to Aiden.

I couldn't hang out at Jade's place forever, no matter how nice it might be.

My best friend's home wasn't as big as Aiden's. It was more of an adorable cottage that was bright with beach themes.

I dropped a pod into her coffeemaker and waited for the finished product.

I'd have to find another apartment, and it would tap my already-dry resources, but I'd figure something out. I always did. Since the restaurant wasn't active and making money, things would be tight for me and Maya, but it wasn't like we weren't used to making do with whatever we could afford.

But I *couldn't afford* to not be working to get the restaurant back up and running.

I need to focus.

No matter what happened between Aiden and me, the last thing I wanted was for Maya to lose her father again. She already loved Aiden so much, and she'd be devastated if he just walked out of her life. So I'd get to Aiden's place shortly, and try to get him to at least commit to maintaining a relationship with Maya until the tests could be redone.

I let out a long sigh as I put cream and sweetener in my coffee. Really, I wanted to go back to bed and pull the covers over my head. Pretend that last night had never happened.

I wanted . . . Aiden.

He'd become my place of safety. Not his house. *Him.* And it had become pure hell to not be able to talk to him when I was feeling down. Or when I was feeling good.

It was torment to not have him near me . . . period.

I tried to blink back the tears that filled my eyes, but my emotions were wide open and exposed now. That psyche trick just didn't work anymore.

Aiden had opened that door, and I couldn't close it.

I loved him, and I was completely screwed.

If I was really honest with myself, I'd admit that I'd *always* loved him. Probably always would. We were connected in a way that just didn't happen every day.

I knew that because he'd been the only man I'd ever loved. The only guy who could make me feel this damn miserable. The one who could also make me unbelievably happy.

Sweeping at the tears pouring down my face, I tried to be strong. I was going to have to pull myself together for my daughter.

She was really going to need me to be there if her father wasn't.

I startled when I heard somebody pounding on the door at the back of the house.

Putting my coffee down, I headed in that direction, wondering if I should even answer it.

I was staying in Jade's house. It was probably a friend or acquaintance of hers. But something drew me to the back entrance, and I pulled the door open anyway.

Aiden!

He was here.

He was real.

My heart was racing as I stared at him like he was some kind of illusion.

He looked like he'd been dragged through the depths of hell, judging by his weary face.

He slammed through the door. "You're here. Jesus Christ! I only checked here out of desperation."

"J-Jade said I could use her place if I wanted. And I didn't really have a place to go," I explained.

"So your car is in the garage?" he guessed.

"Yes."

"You've been this damn close and I didn't know it?"

He started to chuckle. And it wasn't because he was amused. It sounded very much like he was laughing at himself.

"Aiden, what's wrong with you?" He looked wiped out, and I was getting worried.

"I've been all over the city at least three times, Skye, and I've called and texted you like crazy," he growled. "I've searched every lodging for your vehicle. It was the only thing I had to figure out where the hell you went. Why did you leave?"

"You were angry," I said. "And I didn't want Maya to get upset if you slipped up and said something about the tests. I turned my phone off because Maya will answer it if I'm not right next to her."

"I was a fucking idiot, Skye. I should have stayed. I should have just talked it out with you. Instead, I ended up bending my brother's ear for a couple of hours."

He went to Seth's.

Not for a minute had I believed he was trolling for another woman, but it was a relief to know he had gone somewhere innocuous.

I pushed on his shoulder. "Sit. I'll get you some coffee. We need to talk."

He ran a hand over his face. "I've had too much already."

But he did plop his butt on a chair at the table before he added, "I've been looking for you since last night."

I grabbed my own coffee, got him a bottle of water from the fridge, and sat down across from him. "All night?" I questioned.

No wonder he looked like he hadn't slept. He'd probably never gotten to bed.

He nodded, his eyes devouring me like I was some kind of rare treasure. "All morning, too. I was afraid something had happened to you. Don't ever do that shit to me again. I probably deserved it for being an asshole, but you took ten years off my life. Maya okay?"

I inclined my head. "She's fine. She's at school."

"She's my daughter," he said in a rush. "I don't give a damn what the test says, I feel it in here." He pounded on his chest twice. "It doesn't matter if we don't have the same genes. I don't give a shit. And I know there has to be a good reason why you said she was mine. Talk to me, Skye. Explain, like I never gave you a chance to do last night. I shouldn't have left. We'll get through this if you swear never to lie to me again."

He's actually going to give me another chance? He's willing to accept Maya as his daughter even though he thinks she's not biologically related?

I was stunned, and my tears were falling freely down my cheeks all over again.

"Are you as in love with me as I am with you?" I asked before I could censor my words.

His eyes were wild as he answered, "Crazy in love, Skye. Insanely in love with you. We have to work this shit out or I'm not going to be any use to anybody ever again. It's that bad."

I started to bawl like a child. "I love you that way, too."

Aiden got up and lifted me out of my chair, and then took us to the living room. He sat on the couch with me sprawled on his lap.

I sobbed tears of relief onto his chest, letting him shoulder the pain that had been eating me up.

He stroked my back, murmuring incoherent words of comfort in my ear.

Years of pain, fear, and sorrow were being released, and I couldn't stop. I cried until all of those negative emotions were completely gone.

And Aiden did nothing except support me.

It was crazy that he seemed willing to accept me, even if I had lied to him about Maya.

But once I'd calmed down, I couldn't let him continue to think she wasn't really his daughter. "I called the lab," I said in a voice weak from having cried for several minutes straight.

"Then you have the test results?" he asked. "I wanted to call them, but I couldn't find the papers, and I really didn't give a shit because I was too worried about you and Maya."

I moved back so I could see his face.

Everything I'd ever dreamed about was there in his eyes.

His commitment.

His desperation.

And his unconditional love.

"Maya *is* your biological daughter, Aiden. The lab thinks they swapped two samples and labeled them incorrectly. Another guy called them. A man who matched and shouldn't have. He's sure the child isn't his, but he just needed the paperwork to confirm it. Your samples came in on the same day. The results you got were probably his. And he got yours. You need to do a retest, and so does he. But I swear on my life that I was never with anybody but you. And that I was already pregnant when I left for San Diego. It's not possible for her to be anyone else's child."

I could see that he was listening this time, and his gaze was tormented.

"Fuck!" he cursed. "How does that shit happen? And how the hell can I ever make something like that up to you? I called you a liar, Skye."

I shrugged. "Human error. And if you love me, I give you a pass. I'm not always rational when it comes to you, either. And it meant the world to me that you'd accept Maya even if you knew she wasn't your biological child."

"She's a perfect kid. Why wouldn't I? I love her, too."

I nearly went into another crying phase, but I managed to force myself to hold it back this time. "So you believe me now?"

He nodded. "I've got my head on straight now. I shouldn't have ever doubted it in the first place. Tell me what I can do to make it up to you. Please," he rasped.

I could feel in my heart that he wasn't doubting what I'd told him. "Just tell me that you love me again," I insisted. "Because I love you so much it hurts."

He gently slid me off his lap, stood, and rummaged in the pocket of his jeans.

When he found what he was looking for, he knelt beside the couch. "I love you, Skye. Probably more than I can ever express in words. I need you in my life forever. Just marry me and put me out of my misery, for God's sake," he rasped.

He popped open the box he was holding and held it out to me.

It was the most beautiful diamond solitaire I'd ever seen.

I was searching for words. "You don't have to do this to try to make up for saying some things you shouldn't have. I was hurt, but I understand why it happened," I said breathlessly.

"I've had this ring in my pocket since we came back from Vegas. That's how bad I wanted you to be mine. And I still do. Maybe worse than I did when I bought it."

"I'm already yours."

"Then maybe *I need* reassurance," he said huskily. "You don't have to start planning the wedding, but wear my ring. When you're ready someday, then we'll get married. I know you've been through hell. And I don't blame you for not wanting another husband. But I swear I'll try to be everything he wasn't."

Maybe he didn't know it, but Aiden was *already* everything my first husband wasn't.

I opened my mouth, but I didn't know how to tell him that there never had been and never would be any comparison.

Aiden was the only man for me and always had been.

"I love you," I said because I couldn't express how I felt in words.

"I love you, too, sweetheart, but could you just say *yes* already?"

I laughed. "Yes. I'll marry you."

I wasn't afraid of marriage anymore. Not with him. Never with Aiden.

"Thank God," he said in a heavy sigh of relief.

He took the ring and tossed the box aside.

It fit perfectly when he slid it onto my finger, and I felt the slightly eerie sense that something had just happened that should have occurred a long time ago.

Like the world had suddenly been righted, and everything was the way the universe had always intended it to be.

CHAPTER 29
Skye

"You have no damn idea how good it is to see that ring on your finger," he said in a hoarse tone as he sat back down on the couch and pulled me into his lap.

I shivered as I saw the band of white gold and the shimmering diamond on my hand. "I think I do," I argued. "I'm ready to marry you, Aiden. Once we get the test results—"

"They don't matter," he interrupted. "I already know how they'll turn out. I know you weren't lying to me, Skye. And if you had, then you would have told me the truth, and had a damn good reason for doing it. I don't know what happened to me. I guess the thought of you betraying me like that sent me into some kind of temporary twilight zone. I'm pretty rational about everything but you."

"I'm over it," I said truthfully.

Aiden and I were going to make our mistakes, and he'd had reason to have reservations about our relationship. Honestly, I was pretty unreasonable about him at times, too.

We had a crazy kind of love. Strong emotions sometimes meant being irrational. But he'd pulled himself together and thought it through, even though he hadn't *at first*.

"You shouldn't be over it," he rumbled.

"So you want to be tortured?" I teased.

"It might make me feel better about losing my shit," he replied. "I said some things that can't be unsaid. You didn't deserve that."

"Love isn't always going to be perfect, Aiden. We're going to have disagreements. We love each other too much not to argue occasionally. We aren't kids anymore. You're stubborn. I'm independent. Those two traits are bound to collide once in a while. But all the things you've done right far outweigh one day of wrong."

"Tell me what I can do to make it up to you," he demanded.

"Kiss me," I insisted.

"Baby, *that's not* torture," he answered as he pulled my head down.

Wet heat flooded my core the moment I felt his soft, warm, silken lips touch mine.

I was lost, and I didn't really care.

The man who was always meant to be mine was now my fiancé after almost a decade of waiting.

I didn't want to waste another damn minute.

I finally lifted my head, even though the separation from him was painful. "Fuck me, Aiden. Show me all of this is real, because I'm not sure I believe it's really happening."

Truth was, it was hard to fathom that he loved me as much as I loved him.

I was flat on my back on the couch before I could take another breath, with Aiden's muscular body on top of me.

I welcomed him by wrapping my legs around his waist.

"Believe it, baby," he said in a rough voice that was full of emotion. "You and I should have been like this years ago. And I'm never giving your beautiful ass up again. I'd walk through fucking fire to find you if you tried to run away."

I tangled my hands in his hair, and then reveled in the feeling of being so close to him. "I'm not going anywhere," I told him with tears in my eyes.

"Don't cry, sweetheart," he demanded. "I never want to see you cry again."

His mouth came down on mine again, and my chest ached as he explored my mouth so thoroughly that I *knew* everything was real.

His kiss was raw, and it stripped me of any defenses I might have had left inside me.

I needed us both naked, our heated skin fused together like we'd never come apart again.

When he finally lifted his head, I moaned in protest.

"I need you naked," he growled.

Every female hormone I had responded.

He stood, and I scrambled up after him.

I reached for the T-shirt he was wearing, in a frenzy of need.

He helped me shuck it, and then pulled my shirt over my head and added it to the place where he'd tossed his on the floor.

"Wait," I said softly. "Please."

He gave me a curious look.

"Let me touch you," I insisted.

Aiden always made it his mission to make me come as many times as possible. He was an alpha male, and I liked that. But it meant that I rarely got the chance to really touch and pleasure him in return.

He always took the lead.

"For once, let me just touch you," I said in a loud whisper, my voice weak as I stared at all that soft skin over well-developed muscles.

The hot look in his eyes singed me, but he stood still like he was waiting for me to make my move.

I reached for the buttons on his jeans and popped them open, my eyes locked with his as I moved my palms over his chest and his six-pack abs.

Aiden was beautifully made, from his mouth-watering body to his strong, masculine facial features and beautiful blue eyes.

"I love the way you feel," I told him as I traced the sexy trail of hair that disappeared into his open jeans. "You've always been the hottest guy I've ever seen."

I ran my hand over the incredibly hard bulge under the denim he was wearing, and I heard him take in a sharp breath.

That was all the encouragement I needed to drop to my knees and yank the jeans and his boxer briefs down to his feet.

I let him kick them to the side, and then I wrapped my hand around his length and girth.

"Skye," he said in a feral tone.

"Wait," I said, knowing that he was getting impatient. I could feel the testosterone emanating from his body, and it beckoned to me.

There was something powerful about knowing that I could get him as worked up as he could get me.

I wanted to taste him, and I wanted to get it right, since it was something I hadn't done before.

Aiden's cock might be as hard as diamonds, but I loved the silken softness that covered it, and I let my fingers trail down his length before I leaned forward.

Letting instinct take control, I flicked my tongue out and swiped the bead of moisture at the very tip.

I closed my eyes and savored the taste of him, his essence, and then I took as much of the shaft as I could possibly get into my mouth.

"I think I just fucking died," he groaned.

Encouraged, I wrapped my hand around the

root of his cock, and sucked as I pulled back.

I got lost in the rhythm after that, relishing every sound of pleasure he made, and the sensation of his hands grasping my hair in desperation.

I was startled when he moved back suddenly. "You have to stop, Skye, or I'll end up coming in your mouth," he rasped.

I looked up at him. "Would that be so bad?"

"It would be like a wet dream for me, sweetheart. But I need to be inside you right now. I need to feel like all this is real, too. Like you're real."

He pulled me upright and slowly removed the rest of my clothing, dropping each item on the floor.

Entranced, I watched him do it until I was as nude as he was.

"I need you." The words tumbled out of my mouth.

He flopped onto the huge leather sofa. "You have me. You've always had me. Come here."

When I got close enough to the couch, he pulled me down on top of him. I let out a sigh of satisfaction as I straddled him.

"Ride me, beautiful," he said in a hoarse voice.

Our eyes locked, and there was a silent communication that floored me.

He wanted me to keep control. He wanted me to take what I wanted.

And I didn't hesitate as I grasped his cock and positioned the silken head at my entrance.

Sinking down onto him was one of the most incredible things I'd ever felt.

Aiden filled me, stretched me, made me feel complete, and it was breathtaking.

I was so wet that I took him balls-deep pretty easily.

"This is what I needed," I panted. "This. You. Us."

He put his hands on my hips. "Ride me before I lose my damn mind."

There was tension in his expression, but there was also love and passion. And I fed on those emotions.

I lifted up, and then sank down again. The slow, sultry rhythm soon turned into a frantic need to go faster. Take him deeper.

"Aiden," I moaned.

He grasped my hips harder, and started moving up every time I came down.

I let go when the fevered pace got crazy, and my body was screaming for release.

Aiden held me still and pummeled up into me, each stroke harder than the last.

When he shifted positions slightly, and each thrust put pressure on my clit, I came apart.

My climax barreled into me with so much force that I could hardly stay upright.

"Yes," I hissed. "I love you. I love you so much."

Those words got me pulled down for a delirious

kiss, and our mouths met like we'd die if they didn't.

He smothered the moans that I couldn't hold back while my entire body shuddered with my release.

His body quieted after he orgasmed deep inside me seconds later.

When I drew back and put my head on his shoulder, he huffed, "I love you, too, Skye."

I was out of breath, and my heart was galloping, but I smiled against his damp skin.

He stroked a hand up and down my back, and we didn't speak, the sound of our frenetic breathing the only sound in the room until we'd both recovered.

Finally, I said, "When Jade said I could use her place, I'm pretty sure she didn't mean I could use it this way."

Aiden laughed, a sound so low and loud that it seemed to echo through the room. "I'll clean the couch. Or buy her a new one. And I doubt she'd care."

"I'm not telling her," I said quickly.

There was no way I was going to tell my best friend that I'd nailed her brother on her leather couch.

"Let's go home. We have a perfectly good bed there," he said in a sexy baritone that had me scrambling to my feet.

I was sold. I certainly wasn't using Jade's bed to do anything except sleep.

"I have a home now," I murmured. "I don't really know what that's like, Aiden."

Home should be somewhere that a person felt safe. I'd never had that, even in my late mother's house. Maybe that was why I was suddenly longing to be back at Aiden's house.

It was home because we were happy there.

He put his arms around me and pulled me close. "I'll never be home unless you're there. I love you, Skye. I'm so damn sorry about what happened."

I shook my head. "Don't be. We're both going to make some mistakes, Aiden. Just cut me a break when I do something totally irrational in the future."

I put my arms around his neck, basking in the feel of his naked body against mine.

He shook his head. "I'll never make that mistake again. My goal is to make sure you're happy."

"Mission accomplished," I teased. "I'm already there."

"It gets better," he insisted with a grin.

He kissed me, and I melted against him.

I couldn't imagine that life could be any better than it was right now.

CHAPTER 30
Seth

I was tired of women throwing themselves at me.

Okay. I admit it. That's not the thing a typical guy would say, but my circumstances were completely different from the average male's.

One: I was newly wealthy after being poor my entire life.

Two: I was busting my ass to prove I deserved to be a billionaire.

Three: I'd always been too damn busy to date.

Not to mention the fact that I hadn't met any woman who had enticed me to ask her out on a date in the last year or so.

Maybe my dry spell was because I knew that every single woman who approached me only cared about the fact that I had money. Lots of money. And I knew that none of them would have looked at me twice when I'd been a construction worker.

"Are you Seth Sinclair?" a female voice queried.

I cringed as I looked up at the pretty brunette who was holding a cup of coffee—which wasn't unusual since we were in a coffee shop. But her smile was way too hopeful and artificial.

"Yes," I answered abruptly, hoping she'd get the message.

I turned my eyes back to the laptop in front of me. I'd hoped to get my fix of caffeine and accomplish some work at the same time.

"Can I sit here?" she asked with way too much enthusiasm.

I didn't say anything as I looked back at her.

Jesus! My mother, who was long dead now, had raised her sons to be polite. It wasn't really all that easy for me to be a complete jerk—which was something all my siblings would deny. They'd say I was the biggest jackass among them. But I *did* find it difficult to be downright rude to any female.

"Sorry I'm late," a second female voice said as she nudged past the dark-haired woman waiting for me to answer.

I watched as a gorgeous redhead seated herself at my table like she belonged there.

"Sorry, my mistake." The dark-haired woman's voice was brittle, but she turned and walked away.

I turned my attention to the redhead now that the brunette had scurried away.

My new tablemate shrugged the bag off her shoulder and pulled out a laptop computer from it, and then she set it on the table and opened the screen.

She didn't say a word as she started to work,

the quick clicking of the keys telling me that she was furiously doing some kind of project.

Strangely, she didn't appear to be interested in a conversation.

So why in the hell had she sat down at my table like I knew her?

I looked around the coffee shop. There were plenty of tables available, which made her actions even more perplexing.

But really, did it matter *why* she was sitting here? The woman had given me exactly what I wanted.

I had a female at my table, so nobody else was going to approach me.

And she obviously wasn't interested in me personally.

Perfect.

I took a slug of my extra-large coffee and went back to working on my computer.

Problem was, my mind suddenly wasn't on my work—which was way out of character for me.

Building my business was my priority.

I stewed for a moment before I got impatient.

Okay. I *had* to know. "Why did you decide to sit here at my table?"

She didn't stop working, her head still buried in her computer, as she replied, "I was helping you. You're welcome."

My brows drew together. "How were you helping me?" I ignored her sarcastic jab.

301

"You obviously needed a decoy. I needed to sit and work."

I closed my computer, and then reached out and lowered hers, too, so I could see her face.

She frowned at me, something I found vaguely amusing. "I have to work," she said, sounding disgusted.

"Humor me," I requested. "Why did you think I needed help?"

"You looked pretty desperate to escape the runway-model look-alike. I could see the panic on your face."

"I don't panic," I drawled.

"Would you feel better if I said you looked . . . concerned?"

"Yes."

"Good. Then you looked concerned. Can I get back to work now?"

I ignored her request. "So you just took it upon yourself to come rescue me?"

"Yes," she answered sharply.

"Do you do that often?"

"Hardly ever. You were an exception. I have enough problems. I usually let people deal with their own issues. But you did look a little bit desperate."

I leaned back in my chair. The female was attractive. Okay, maybe she was beautiful. Honestly, I'd say she was *striking*, too.

Her hazel eyes were inquisitive and bright, and

even though her fiery hair was pulled up and secured to the back of her head, small tendrils framed a face with gorgeous features.

She was dressed for success in an A-line black skirt, a white blouse, and a matching dark jacket. I hadn't seen her feet, but I was willing to bet she was wearing sensible heels.

Who knew that a woman in a suit could be such a turn-on?

And the female *was* smoking hot. I had a feeling it didn't much matter what she was wearing.

Maybe the part I liked about her the best was her lack of interest in me.

"I have my own difficulties, too," I mused. "And I generally don't butt into anybody else's business."

"You should try it sometime," she suggested. "It makes you forget your own drama for a while. It's a stress reliever. So what are you struggling with today?"

I raised an eyebrow. "Do you really want to know?"

"Not really," she answered. "But I am sitting at your table. So shoot."

I had to force myself not to smile. The woman was brutally honest. But she intrigued me. And that was something I hadn't experienced for a long time. "I'm a builder, and I have a pain-in-the-ass tree hugger who is keeping me from building on a site because it's the nesting place

303

for some endangered birds. It could cost me millions of dollars if the site can't be built on."

She shook her head. "Sounds horrible," she commented. "So you're a builder?"

I inclined my head. "I'm Seth Sinclair. I own Sinclair Properties."

She didn't look the least bit impressed.

"I've heard of you. Didn't you inherit billions of dollars? The story was all over the local news. You're connected to the Boston Sinclairs, right?"

She still looked unfazed, which I found confusing. Most women's attitudes changed immediately once they knew who I was and how much money I had.

The woman was kind of an enigma. I couldn't even sense what she was thinking.

"They're half-siblings and cousins," I explained.

"So why do you want to build on a site that houses a threatened species?" she asked.

"Because I own it," I drawled.

"I kind of think the birds were probably there first," she replied.

"I'll lose millions if I don't build. I'm not just going to donate expensive coastal land."

"I doubt you'd really miss the money," she contemplated. "And if you're getting that much resistance, why don't you just give it up? There's a lot of other places to build. But you can't bring back extinct animals."

I let out an exasperated sigh. "You're starting to sound just like my sister Jade."

"I don't know her personally, but she seems like an amazing woman," she answered. "She's done some incredible work on conservation genetics. I admire your sister, actually. So I don't mind sounding like her."

I watched as the woman put her computer away.

"Don't rush away on my account," I said, unsettled that the female was going to leave as quickly as she'd arrived.

"I've done my good deed for the day."

"I'm kind of enjoying the conversation."

She shot me a puzzled look. "Why? I obviously don't agree with you."

I shrugged. "Maybe that's why I like it."

"You don't have friends with different opinions?"

I shook my head. "Not really. I don't actually have many real friends."

My best friends were my brothers. I'd never had much time to socialize. My priority had always been my family, and working hard to make sure we weren't separated.

"What a shocker," she said sarcastically as she zipped up her computer bag. "A generous guy like you should be surrounded by friends."

"You're mocking me," I said with surprise.

"Look, I don't really know you. But it seems to me like you're the kind of guy who places more

305

value on money than on your environment. So it's almost impossible for me to take you seriously."

"It's not that I don't care about the birds," I told her honestly. "I just think losing millions of dollars over it is kind of ridiculous."

She stood up and buttoned her suit jacket. "I have to go. I wish I could say it was a pleasure to meet you, but it really wasn't."

I actually flinched from the insult. "I don't understand why you're so adamant about a bunch of birds," I grumbled.

"Maybe because my name is Riley Montgomery," she shot back as she hefted her bag onto her shoulder. "I'm a big part of your *annoying problem*."

I gaped at her as she turned and walked away without another word.

I couldn't move my eyes from the sway of that sexy, shapely ass as she disappeared.

When I finally blinked, she was gone.

I smiled even though she'd pretty much gotten one over on me.

And she was the last woman who should get my dick hard, but I couldn't deny that she had.

"I'll be damned," I said under my breath.

I'd just met and gotten shot down by my annoying tree hugger.

EPILOGUE
Skye

A few weeks later . . .

"Open it," I told Aiden as we sat at his kitchen table around two weeks after I'd become his fiancée.

I was eager to have the question of Maya's parentage done and over with, even though Aiden had insisted that he no longer had any doubts.

The last few weeks had been so amazing, but for me, there were always those incorrect lab results looming like an annoying dark cloud over my head.

Maya and Aiden had done a retest, and the laboratory had put a rush on the results.

And now that they had arrived, I was dying to have the real truth out in the open.

I wanted to close that door for good and move on.

"I already know what they're going to say," he said as he grinned at me. "This one is a definite winner." He pointed at his empty plate.

I rolled my eyes. "Forget the latest sandwich for a minute."

"Can't," he argued. "It has to be on the menu."

"Aiden," I said in a warning voice.

He shrugged. "If you're so interested, you can open it. I have absolutely no doubt what it says. No suspense for me."

I bit my lip, tempted. "They're your results."

"Hey," he said, sounding concerned. "You look upset. Are you okay, sweetheart?"

There was no joking around now that he saw tension on my face.

"Just open it. I guess I just want to put this all behind us."

"It *is* behind us, Skye. But since it bothers you, I'll look."

He grabbed the sealed envelope on the table and ripped it open.

It drove me crazy that it took him a couple of minutes to get to the conclusion.

"It says I'm Maya's father with 99.999 percent accuracy." He handed the paperwork over. "Happy now?"

I went straight to the conclusion, and then I smiled at him. "Yes. Thank you for not doubting the results. But I wasn't going to rest until you saw it for yourself."

"If nothing else, it's pretty mind blowing to see it in writing, although I'm still not used to being a dad. Is it normal to worry this much?" he asked with a frown.

I nodded as I shot him a smile. "Welcome to parenthood. I was scared to death that first year.

Every time she cried, I panicked. But it gets better. And it's easier when you have a kid who has such a good head on her shoulders."

He smirked. "She's pretty incredible. Keeps me on my toes." In a more serious tone, he asked, "Ever think about having another one?"

I glanced up at him sharply. "You want more kids?"

"That all depends on you."

I'd never really thought about having more children until he mentioned it. A few months ago, it hadn't even been on my radar.

But now, I thought it would be an incredible experience to share with Aiden from the beginning next time. And I did love kids. I'd just never considered whether or not I wanted more. I never thought I'd get serious with a man ever again.

He'd be there for everything, every step of the way.

"I think I'd like that," I answered. "When I was younger, I always wanted a big family."

"You're already inheriting one of those," he remarked wryly.

I shot him an admonishing look. "I don't mean that, and I love your family. But I was an only child. It was pretty lonely sometimes. And I love kids. Maya would be ecstatic if she could have a brother or sister. If I remember right, she already put in the request for one."

His expression was deliciously wicked as he answered, "Then by all means, let's give her a couple. I'm ready to start practicing right now."

I let go of a delighted laugh. "Not so fast, mister. I'm going to be married before I get pregnant again, and you still need time to get used to having a daughter."

He reached over and started to toy with my beautiful engagement ring. "When you're ready."

"I am ready, Aiden. I'm all in. Now that you've seen the results, I'm putting my past behind me because right now is extraordinary, and my future will be, too. I'd much rather focus on that than my past. Let's just go to the courthouse and do it."

He got to his feet, pulled me up, and then swung me around until I was dizzy. "I'm getting married," he bellowed.

When he stopped twirling me, I smacked his arm playfully. "I told you I was ready."

"But I don't think I really believed it until now," he said huskily.

I knew why he felt that way. Probably because I'd been feeling unsettled since the new lab results weren't in. "Believe it," I said, repeating the words he said to me when I was overwhelmed.

"No courthouse," he insisted. "I've waited almost a decade for this."

"Me too," I said as I stroked a lock of hair from his forehead. "But I guess I just never imagined it would ever happen."

"Believe it," he parroted with a grin.

"You do realize that if we have a regular wedding, there won't be anybody on the bride's side?"

"Baby, *everybody* will be on your side. And that's a dumb tradition anyway. People can sit wherever they want. My family is yours now, whether you want them or not."

"I want them," I said quickly. "Maya and I have been lonely long enough. We've always had each other, but I've always *wished* she had other family, too. Your daughter adores her new aunts, uncles, and cousins. She's happier than she's ever been."

I loved the animated look on Maya's face when she talked about her family.

Aiden and I had been careful not to share why we'd argued, and my offspring had never asked. She'd just been happy when everything was *normal* again in her eyes.

He tightened his arms around my waist. "Then let's shoot for the end of the summer. Earlier if possible. I'd like to get started on our new life together. We've both had enough of waiting, and I want you to be able to focus on the future. You've had way too much pain in your past, baby."

How could I tell Aiden that he more than made up for every bit of anguish I'd ever suffered at the hands of my ex-husband and his family? I'd do it all over again if I had to in order to end up where

I was right now. Nine years of hell in exchange for total happiness for the rest of my life? I'd do that deal in a heartbeat if I could finally be married to the only man I'd ever love.

"End of summer would only give me four months to plan," I contemplated.

"Plenty of time when you have a ton of family members to help out," he answered with a grin.

"Jade has to stand up for me. I'll talk to her, since she already has wedding connections, and then start planning," I promised.

He rested his forehead on mine. "And then I can seriously work on getting you knocked up," he teased. "But I'll practice a lot before then so I'm perfect at it when the time comes. I think I want you and our daughter to myself for a while."

I let out a startled laugh. "You're not going to hear me argue about that," I teased.

I wanted another child, but like him, I needed some time before I'd be ready to add to our family. I wanted our daughter to be secure with her place in our life, and I knew that Aiden wanted to try to catch up with everything he'd missed in Maya's life.

He stroked my hair as he said, "I wish I would have been there for Maya's birth. But I'll be there next time."

I sighed as I laid my head on his shoulder, delighting in the warmth of his body plastered to mine.

I refused to lament over the things we'd missed by not being together. I was too happy about how they'd all worked out in the end. "I love you, Aiden. I'm so happy that we ended up like this, even though it took far too long."

"I think I've always been waiting for you, Skye. Nobody else was ever going to make me happy," he said in a voice raw with emotion.

"I'm glad you waited," I whispered in his ear.

Nobody else would have made me happy, either. All my life, there had only ever been *him*.

"I don't think I had much choice. I was as in love with you then as I am now."

"Why didn't you ever tell me?"

"You must have known."

"But you never said it. I told you that I loved you before you left, but you never said it to me."

"Didn't I?" he asked.

I shook my head against his shoulder. "No. I was kind of heartbroken because you didn't say it back. I thought it was just too soon."

"Maybe it was because I knew I had nothing to offer you," he answered solemnly. "I was a poor fisherman, Skye. What kind of life would you have had with me?"

I leaned back so I could look him in the eyes. "A happy one," I guessed. "Aiden, I didn't care about that. Money doesn't bring happiness."

He shook his head. "It doesn't hurt."

"You were still the same amazing guy back then that you are now."

"Do you really think I could have gone forever without saying it?" he teased. "Eventually, we would have ended up together, because I sure as hell wouldn't have given you up. I would have just worked harder and let you grow up until you realized what you'd be taking on. *And then* I would have married you. I might be stubborn about wanting you to have what I think you deserve. But I wasn't stupid enough to let you walk away."

"I didn't plan on going anywhere, then or now. I didn't care about the money. I just wanted . . . you," I murmured as I tightened my arms around his neck.

My heart was aching with elation because this beautiful man was finally mine forever.

A miracle I thought would never happen.

"You're stuck with me now, sweetheart," he joked. "I'm never letting go."

Our eyes locked, the connection between us exchanging messages without words.

It was like that with Aiden. We usually knew what the other person was thinking.

"Take me to bed, Aiden. Maya won't be home for another two hours."

He gave me that lazy smile that always made my heart skitter with anticipation.

"You're getting bossy now," he mused.

"You have a problem with that?" I challenged.

I'd become much more sexually bold, and I was pretty sure he was completely on board with that.

"Nope. Not at all," he answered as he picked me up and swung me into his arms. "I think I can handle it."

I had no doubt he could cope with anything I threw in his direction, which was one of the reasons I loved him so damn much.

"I love you, Aiden." I couldn't seem to keep the words contained. I could say it a million times and it wouldn't be enough.

"I love you," he said, the sincerity of those words expressed in his magnificent eyes.

I savored those three little words as he carried me into the bedroom, the words he *hadn't said* when we were younger.

I was all grown up now, and I could never hear them enough.

ACKNOWLEDGMENTS

I hope you all enjoyed Aiden and Skye's story as much as I enjoyed writing it.

As always, I want to thank all the crew at Montlake for all their support of The Accidental Billionaires, and Senior Editor Maria Gomez for believing in this series.

Huge appreciation to my reader group and street team, Jan's Gems, for helping me spread the word about this series.

I want to thank my own KA team and my incredible husband, Sri, for all they do to promote each and every book.

Lastly, a huge thank-you to my readers for all their support. I'm incredibly grateful that I can continue to do what I love full time.

An author is only as good as the team of people behind them. I think I'm pretty lucky to have so many amazing people in my corner.

xxxxxxxxx Jan

ABOUT THE AUTHOR

J. S. "Jan" Scott is the *New York Times* and *USA Today* bestselling author of numerous contemporary and paranormal romances, including The Sinclairs and The Accidental Billionaires series. She's an avid reader of all types of books and literature, but romance has always been her genre of choice—so she writes what she loves to read: stories that are almost always steamy, generally feature an alpha male, and have a happily ever after, because she just can't seem to write them any other way! Jan loves to connect with readers. Visit her website at www.authorjsscott.com.

Center Point Large Print
600 Brooks Road / PO Box 1
Thorndike, ME 04986-0001 USA

(207) 568-3717

US & Canada:
1 800 929-9108
www.centerpointlargeprint.com